THE NOVELS OF
IVAN TURGENEV
VOLUME XII

A LEAR OF
THE STEPPES

AND OTHER STORIES

BY

the Novels of

IVAN TURGENEV

Translated from the Russian

By CONSTANCE GARNETT

LONDON

WILLIAM HEINEMANN

1898

AMS PRESS
NEW YORK

Reprinted with permission of William Heinemann Limited and the
 Constance Garnett Estate
From the edition of 1894–1899
First AMS EDITION published 1970
Manufactured in the United States of America

PG 3421
.A 15
1970
V. 12

Library of Congress Catalog Card Number: 70-104348

SBN: complete set: 404-01900-5
volume 12: 404-01912-9

AMS PRESS, INC.
NEW YORK, N.Y. 10003

INTRODUCTION

I

AN examination of *A Lear of the Steppes* is of especial interest to authors, as the story is so exquisite in its structure, so overwhelming in its effects, that it exposes the artificiality of the great majority of the clever works of art in fiction. *A Lear of the Steppes* is great in art because it is a living organic whole, springing from the deep roots of life itself; and the innumerable works of art that are fabricated and pasted together from an ingenious plan— works that do not grow from the inevitability of things—appear at once insignificant or false in comparison.

In examining the art, the artist will note that Turgenev's method of introducing his story is a lesson in sincerity. Harlov, the Lear of the story, is brought forward with such force on the threshold that all eyes resting on his figure

v

cannot but follow his after movements. And absolute conviction gained, all the artist's artful after-devices and subtle presentations and side-lights on the story are not apparent under the straightforward ease and the seeming careless-ness with which the narrator describes his boyish memories. Then, Harlov's household, his two daughters, and a crowd of minor characters, are brought before us as persons in the tragedy, and we see that all these people are living each from the innate laws of his being, *apparently independently of the author's scheme.* This conviction, that the author has no pre-arranged plan, convinces us that in the story we are living a piece of life : here we are verily plunging into life itself.

And the story goes on flowing easily and natur-ally till the people of the neighbourhood, the peasants, the woods and fields around, are known by us as intimately as is any neighbourhood in life. Suddenly a break—the tragedy is upon us. Suddenly the terrific forces that underlie human life, even the meanest of human lives, burst on us astonished and breathless, pre-cisely as a tragedy comes up to the surface and bursts on us in real life : everybody runs about dazed, annoyed, futile ; we watch the other people sustaining their own individuality inadequately in the face of the monstrous new events which go their fatal way logically, events which leave the people huddled and useless and gasping. And destruction having burst out of life, life slowly returns to its old grooves —with a difference to us, the difference in the relation of people one to another that a death or a tragedy always leaves to the survivors. Marvellous in its truth is Turgenev's analysis of the situation after Harlov's death, marvellous is the simple description of the neighbourhood's attitude to the Harlov family, and marvellous is the lifting of the scene on the after-life of Harlov's daughters. In the pages (pages 140, 141, 146, 147) on these women, Turgenev flashes into the reader's mind an extraordinary sense of the inevitability of these women's natures, of their innate growth fashioning their after-lives as logically as a beech puts out beech-leaves and an oak oak-leaves. Through Turgenev's single glimpse at their fortunes one knows the whole intervening fifteen years ; he has carried us into a new world : yet it is the old world ; one needs to know no more. It is life arbitrary but inevitable, life so clarified by art that it is absolutely interpreted ; but life with all the sense of mystery that nature breathes around it in its ceaseless growth.

II

This sense of inevitability and of the mystery of life which Turgenev gives us in *A Lear of the Steppes* is the highest demand we can make from art. *Acia*, the last story in the present volume, though it gives us a sense of mystery, is not inevitable : the end is *faked* to suit the artist's purpose, and thus, as in other ways, it is far inferior to *Lear*. *Faust*, the second story, has consummate charm in its strange atmosphere of the supernatural mingling with things earthly, but it is not, as is *Lear*, life seen from the surface to the revealed depths ; it is a revelation of the strange forces in life, presented beautifully; but it is rather an idea, a problem to be worked out by certain characters, than a piece of life inevitable and growing. When an artist creates in us the sense of inevitability, then his work is at its highest, and is obeying nature's law of growth, unfolding from out itself as inevitably as a tree or a flower or a human being unfolds from out itself. Turgenev at his highest never quits nature, yet he always uses the surface, and what is apparent, to disclose her most secret principles, her deepest potentialities, her inmost laws of being, and whatever he presents he presents clearly and simply. This combination of powers marks only the few supreme artists. Even great masters often fail in perfect *naturalness*: Tolstoi's *The Death of Ivan Ilytch*, for example, one of the most powerful stories ever written, has too little that is typical of the whole of life, too much that is strained towards the general purpose of the story, to be really *natural*. Turgenev's special feat in fiction is that his characters reveal themselves by the most ordinary details of their every-day life; and while these details are always giving us the whole life of the people, and their inner life as well, the novel's significance is being built up simply out of these details, built up by the same process, in fact, as nature creates for us a single strong impression out of a multitude of little details. The Impressionists, it is true, often give us amazingly clever pictures of life, seen subtly and drawn naturally; but, in general, their able pictures of the way men think and act do not reveal more than the actual thinking and acting that men betray to one another,— they do not betray the whole significance of their lives more than does the daily life itself. And so the Impressionists give pictures of life's surface, and not interpretations of its eternal depths: they pass away as portraits of the

time, amazingly felicitous artistic portraits.
But Turgenev's power as a poet comes in,
whenever he draws a commonplace figure, to
make it bring with it a sense of the mystery
of its existence. In *Lear* the steward Kvitsinsky
plays a subsidiary part; he has apparently no
significance in the story, and very little is told
about him. But who does not perceive that
Turgenev looks at and presents the figure of
this man in a manner totally different from the
way any clever novelist of the second rank
would look at and use him? Kvitsinsky, in
Turgenev's hands, is an individual with all the
individual's mystery in his glance, his coming
and going, his way of taking things; but he is
a part of the household's breath, of its very
existence; he breathes the atmosphere naturally
and creates an atmosphere of his own. If
Hugo had created him he would have been
out of focus immediately; Balzac would have
described the household minutely, and then let
Kvitsinsky appear as a separate entity in it;
the Impressionists would sketch him as a living
picture, a part of the household, but he would
remain as first created, he would always repeat
the first impression he makes on us, a certain man
in a certain aspect; and they would not give us
the steward revealing his character imperceptibly

from day to day in his minute actions, naturally, and little by little, as this man reveals his.

It is then in his marvellous sense of the growth of life that Turgenev is superior to most of his rivals. Not only did he observe life minutely and comprehensively, but he reproduces it as a constantly growing phenomenon, growing naturally, not accidentally or arbitrarily. For example, in *A House of Gentle-folk*, take Lavretsky's and Liza's changes of mood when they are falling in love one with another: it is nature herself in them changing very delicately and insensibly; we feel that the whole picture is alive, not an effect cut out from life, and cut off from it at the same time, like a bunch of cut flowers, an effect which many clever novelists often give us. And in *Lear* we feel that the life in Harlov's village is still going on, growing yonder, still growing with all its mysterious sameness and changes, when, in Turgenev's last words, 'The story-teller ceased, and we talked a little longer, and then parted, each to his home.'

III

Turgenev's sympathy with women and his unequalled power of drawing them, not merely as they appear to men, but as they appear to each other, has been dwelt on by many writers. And in truth, of the three leading qualities into which his artistic powers may be arbitrarily analysed, the most apparent is precisely that delicate feminine intuition and sensitive emotional consciousness into all the nuances of personal relations that women possess in life and are never able to put into books. This fluid sympathetic perception is instinctive in Turgenev: it is his temperament to be sympathetic or receptive to all types, except, perhaps, to purely masculine men of action, whom he never draws with success. His temperament is bathed in a delicate emotional atmosphere quivering with light, which discloses all the infinite riches of the created world, the relation of each character to its particular universe, and the significance of its human fate. And this state of soul or flow of mood in Turgenev is creative, as when music floats from a distance to the listener, immediately the darkening fields, the rough coarse earth of cheap human life, with all the grind and petty monotony of existence, melt into harmony, and life is seen as a mysterious whole, not merely as a puzzling discrepancy of gaps and contradictions and days of little import. This fluid emotional consciousness of Turgenev is feminine, inasmuch as it is a receptive, sympathising, and harmonising attitude; but just where the woman's faculty of receptiveness ends, where her perception fails to go beyond the facts she is alive to, Turgenev's consciousness flashes out into the great poet's creative world, with its immense breadth of vision, force, and imagination. Thus in laying down *A Lear of the Steppes* the reader is conscious that he is seeing past the human life of the tragedy on to the limitless seas of existence beyond,—he is looking beyond the heads of the moving human figures out on to the infinite horizon. Just where the woman's interest would stop and rest satisfied with the near personal elements in the drama, Turgenev's constructive poetic force sees the universal, and in turn interprets these figures in relation to the far wider field of the race, the age, and makes them symbolical of the deep forces of all human existence.

And thus Turgenev becomes a creator, originating a world greater than he received. His creation of Bazarov in *Fathers and Children* from a three hours' accidental meeting with a man while on a journey, is an extraordinary instance of how unerringly his vision created in forethought a world that was to come. He accepted the man, he was penetrated with the new and strange conceptions of life offered, and as a poet he saw in a flash the immense significance to society of this man's appearance in the age. He saw a new and formidable type had arisen in the nation, negating its traditions, its beliefs, its conceptions; and from this solitary meeting with an individual, Turgenev laid bare and predicted the progress of the most formidable social and political movement in modern Russia, predicted it and set it forth in art, a decade before its birth.

IV

In truth, Turgenev's art at its highest may well be the despair of artists who have sufficient insight to understand wherein he excels. He is rich in all the gifts, so he penetrates into everything; but it is the perfect harmony existing between his gifts that makes him see everything in proportion. Thus he never caricatures; he is never too forcible, and never too clever. He is a great realist, and his realism carries along with it the natural breath of poetry. His art is highly complex, but its expression is so pellucid, so simple, that we can see only its body, never the mechanism of its body. His thought and his emotion are blended in one; he interprets life, but always preserves the atmosphere, the glamour, the mystery of the living thing in his interpretation. His creative world arises spontaneously from his own depths—the mark of the world's great masters. Never thinking of himself, he inspires his readers with a secret delight for the beauty that he found everywhere in life. And he never shuts his eyes against the true.

EDWARD GARNETT.

October 1898.

CONTENTS

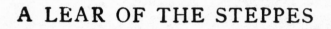

A LEAR OF THE STEPPES

A LEAR OF THE STEPPES

WE were a party of six, gathered together one winter evening at the house of an old college friend. The conversation turned on Shakespeare, on his types, and how profoundly and truly they were taken from the very heart of humanity. We admired particularly their truth to life, their actuality. Each of us spoke of the Hamlets, the Othellos, the Falstaffs, even the Richard the Thirds and Macbeths—the two last only potentially, it is true, resembling their prototypes—whom he had happened to come across.

'And I, gentlemen,' cried our host, a man well past middle age, 'used to know a King Lear!'

'How was that?' we questioned him.

'Oh, would you like me to tell you about him?'

'Please do.'

And our friend promptly began his narrative.

'ALL my childhood,' he began, 'and early youth, up to the age of fifteen, I spent in the country, on the estate of my mother, a wealthy landowner in X—— province. Almost the most vivid impression, that has remained in my memory of that far-off time, is the figure of our nearest neighbour, Martin Petrovitch Harlov. Indeed it would be difficult for such an impression to be obliterated: I never in my life afterwards met anything in the least like Harlov. Picture to yourselves a man of gigantic stature. On his huge carcase was set, a little askew, and without the least trace of a neck, a prodigious head. A perfect hay-stack of tangled yellowish-grey hair stood up all over it, growing almost down to the bushy eyebrows. On the broad expanse of his purple face, that looked as though it had been peeled, there protruded a sturdy knobby nose; diminu-tive little blue eyes stared out haughtily, and a mouth gaped open that was diminutive too, but crooked, chapped, and of the same colour as the rest of the face. The voice that proceeded from this mouth, though hoarse, was exceedingly strong and resonant. . . . Its sound recalled the clank of iron bars, carried in a cart over a badly paved road; and when Harlov spoke, it was as though some one were shouting in a high wind across a wide ravine. It was difficult to tell just what Harlov's face expressed, it was such an expanse. . . . One felt one could hardly take it all in at one glance. But it was not disagreeable—a certain grandeur indeed could be discerned in it, only it was exceedingly astounding and unusual. And what hands he had—positive cushions! What fingers, what feet! I remember I could never gaze without a certain respectful awe at the four-foot span of Martin Petrovitch's back, at his shoulders, like millstones. But what especially struck me was his ears! They were just like great twists of bread, full of bends and curves; his cheeks seemed to support them on both sides. Martin Petrovitch used to wear— winter and summer alike—a Cossack dress of green cloth, girt about with a small Tcherkess strap, and tarred boots. I never saw a cravat on him; and indeed what could he have tied a cravat round? He breathed slowly and heavily, like a bull, but walked without a sound. One might have imagined that having got into a room, he was in constant fear of upsetting and overturning everything, and so moved cautiously from place to place, sideways for the most part, as though slinking by. He was possessed of a strength truly Herculean, and in consequence enjoyed great renown in the neighbourhood. Our common people retain to this day their reverence for Titanic heroes. Legends were invented about him. They used to recount that he had one day met a bear in the forest and had almost vanquished him; that having once caught a thief in his beehouse, he had flung him, horse and cart and all, over the hedge, and so on. Harlov himself never boasted of his strength. 'If my right hand is blessed,' he used to say, 'so it is God's will it should be!' He was proud, only he did not take pride in his strength, but in his rank, his descent, his common sense.

'Our family's descended from the Swede Harlus,' he used to maintain. 'In the princely reign of Ivan Vassilievitch the Dark (fancy how long ago!) he came to Russia, and that Swede Harlus did not wish to be a Finnish count— but he wished to be a Russian nobleman, and he was inscribed in the golden book. It's from him we Harlovs are sprung! . . . And by the same token, all of us Harlovs are born flaxen-haired, with light eyes and clean faces, because we're children of the snow!'

'But, Martin Petrovitch,' I once tried to object, 'there never was an Ivan Vassilievitch the Dark. Then was an Ivan Vassilievitch the

6

Terrible. The Dark was the name given to the great prince Vassily Vassilievitch.'

'What nonsense will you talk next!' Harlov answered serenely; 'since I say so, so it was!'

One day my mother took it into her head to commend him to his face for his really remarkable incorruptibility.

'Ah, Natalia Nikolaevna!' he protested almost angrily; 'what a thing to praise me for, really! We gentlefolk can't be otherwise; so that no churl, no low-born, servile creature dare even imagine evil of us! I am a Harlov, my family has come down from'—here he pointed up somewhere very high aloft in the ceiling—'and me not be honest! How is it possible?'

Another time a high official, who had come into the neighbourhood and was staying with my mother, fancied he could make fun of Martin Petrovitch. The latter had again referred to the Swede Harlus, who came to Russia . . .

'In the days of King Solomon?' the official interrupted.

'No, not of King Solomon, but of the great Prince Ivan Vassilievitch the Dark.'

'But I imagine,' the official pursued, 'that your family is much more ancient, and goes back to antediluvian days, when there were still mastodons and megatheriums about.'

These scientific names were absolutely meaningless to Martin Petrovitch; but he realised that the dignitary was laughing at him.

'May be so,' he boomed, 'our family is, no doubt, very ancient; in those days when my ancestor was in Moscow, they do say there was as great a fool as your excellency living there, and such fools are not seen twice in a thousand years.'

The high official was in a furious rage, while Harlov threw his head back, stuck out his chin, snorted and disappeared. Two days later, he came in again. My mother began reproaching him. 'It's a lesson for him, ma'am,' interposed Harlov, 'not to fly off without knowing what he's about, to find out whom he has to deal with first. He's young yet, he must be taught.' The dignitary was almost of the same age as Harlov; but this Titan was in the habit of regarding every one as not fully grown up. He had the greatest confidence in himself and was afraid of absolutely no one. 'Can they do anything to me? Where on earth is the man that can?' he would ask, and suddenly he would go off into a short but deafening guffaw.

MY mother was exceedingly particular in her choice of acquaintances, but she made Harlov welcome with special cordiality and allowed him many privileges. Twenty-five years before, he had saved her life by holding up her carriage on the edge of a deep precipice, down which the horses had already fallen. The traces and straps of the harness broke, but Martin Petrovitch did not let go his hold of the wheel he had grasped, though the blood spurted out under his nails. My mother had arranged his marriage. She chose for his wife an orphan girl of seventeen, who had been brought up in her house; he was over forty at the time. Martin Petrovitch's wife was a frail creature— they said he carried her into his house in the palms of his hands—and she did not live long with him. She bore him two daughters, how-ever. After her death, my mother continued her good offices to Martin Petrovitch. She placed his elder daughter in the district school, and afterwards found her a husband, and already had another in her eye for the second.

9

Harlov was a fairly good manager. He had a little estate of nearly eight hundred acres, and had built on to his place a little, and the way the peasants obeyed him is indescribable. Owing to his stoutness, Harlov scarcely ever went anywhere on foot: the earth did not bear him. He used to go everywhere in a low racing droshky, himself driving a rawboned mare, thirty years old, with a scar on her shoulder, from a wound which she had received in the battle of Borodino, under the quartermaster of a cavalry regiment. This mare was always somehow lame in all four legs; she could not go at a walking pace, but could only change from a trot to a canter. She used to eat mugwort and wormwood along the hedges, which I have never noticed any other horse do. I remember I always used to wonder how such a broken-down nag could draw such a fearful weight. I won't venture to repeat how many hundred-weight were attributed to our neighbour. In the droshky behind Martin Petrovitch's back perched his swarthy page, Maximka. With his face and whole person squeezed close up to his master, and his bare feet propped on the hind axle bar of the droshky, he looked like a little leaf or worm which had clung by chance to the gigantic carcase before him. This same page boy used once a week to shave Martin Petro-vitch. He used, so they said, to stand on a table to perform this operation. Some jocose

persons averred that he had to run round his
master's chin. Harlov did not like staying
long at home, and so one might often see him
driving about in his invariable equipage, with
the reins in one hand (the other he held
smartly on his knee with the elbow crooked
upwards), with a diminutive old cap on the very
top of his head. He looked boldly about him
with his little bear-like eyes, shouted in a voice
of thunder to all the peasants, artisans, and
tradespeople he met. Priests he greatly dis-
liked, and he would send vigorous abjurations
after them when he met them. One day on
overtaking me (I was out for a stroll with my
gun), he hallooed at a hare that lay near the
road in such a way that I could not get the
roar and ring of it out of my ears all day.

III

My mother, as I have already stated, made Martin Petrovitch very welcome. She knew what a profound respect he entertained for her person. 'She is a real gentlewoman, one of our sort,' was the way he used to refer to her. He used to style her his benefactress, while she saw in him a devoted giant, who would not have hesitated to face a whole mob of peasants in defence of her ; and although no one foresaw the barest possibility of such a contingency, still, to my mother's notions, in the absence of a husband—she had early been left a widow—such a champion as Martin Petrovitch was not to be despised. And besides, he was a man of upright character, who curried favour with no one, never borrowed money or drank spirits ; and no fool either, though he had received no sort of education. My mother trusted Martin Petrovitch : when she took it into her head to make her will, she asked him to witness it, and he drove home expressly to fetch his round iron-rimmed spectacles, without which he could not write. And with spectacles on nose, he

succeeded, in a quarter of an hour, with many
gasps and groans and great effort, in inscribing
his Christian name, father's name, and surname
and his rank and designation, tracing enormous
quadrangular letters, with tails and flourishes.
Having completed this task, he declared he
was tired out, and that writing for him was as
hard work as catching fleas. Yes, my mother
had a respect for him . . . he was not, however,
admitted beyond the dining-room in our house.
He carried a very strong odour about with
him ; there was a smell of the earth, of decaying
forest, of marsh mud about him. 'He's a
forest-demon!' my old nurse would declare.
At dinner a special table used to be laid apart
in a corner for Martin Petrovitch, and he was
not offended at that, he knew other people
were ill at ease sitting beside him, and he too
had greater freedom in eating. And he did
eat too, as no one, I imagine, has eaten since the
days of Polyphemus. At the very beginning
of dinner, by way of a precautionary measure,
they always served him a pot of some four
pounds of porridge, 'else you'd eat me out
of house and home,' my mother used to say.
'That I should, ma'am,' Martin Petrovitch
would respond, grinning.

My mother liked to hear his reflections on
any topic connected with the land. But she
could not support the sound of his voice for
long together. 'What's the meaning of it, my

good sir!' she would exclaim; 'you might take something to cure yourself of it, really! You simply deafen me. Such a trumpet-blast!'

'Natalia Nikolaevna! benefactress!' Martin Petrovitch would rejoin, as a rule, 'I'm not responsible for my throat. And what medicine could have any effect on me—kindly tell me that? I'd better hold my tongue for a bit.'

In reality, I imagine, no medicine could have affected Martin Petrovitch. He was never ill.

He was not good at telling stories, and did not care for it. 'Much talking gives me asthma,' he used to remark reproachfully. It was only when one got him on to the year 1812—he had served in the militia, and had received a bronze medal, which he used to wear on festive occasions attached to a Vladimir ribbon—when one questioned him about the French, that he would relate some few anecdotes. He used, however, to maintain stoutly all the while that there never had been any Frenchmen, real ones, in Russia, only some poor marauders, who had straggled over from hunger, and that he had given many a good drubbing to such rabble in the forests.

IV

AND yet even this self-confident, unflinching giant had his moments of melancholy and depression. Without any visible cause he would suddenly begin to be sad; he would lock himself up alone in his room, and hum— positively hum—like a whole hive of bees; or he would call his page Maximka, and tell him to read aloud to him out of the solitary book which had somehow found its way into his house, an odd volume of Novikovsky's *The Worker at Leisure*, or else to sing to him. And Maximka, who by some strange freak of chance, could spell out print, syllable by syllable, would set to work with the usual chopping up of the words and transference of the accent, bawling out phrases of the following description: 'but man in his wilfulness draws from this empty hypothesis, which he applies to the animal kingdom, utterly opposite conclusions. Every animal separately,' he says, 'is not capable of making me happy!' and so on. Or he would chant in a shrill little voice a mournful song, of which nothing could be distinguished but: 'Ee ... eee ... ee ... a ...

ee . . . a . . . ee . . . Aaa . . . ska! O . . . oo . . .
oo . . . bee . . . ee . . . ee . . . ee . . . la!' While
Martin Petrovitch would shake his head, make
allusions to the mutability of life, how all things
turn to ashes, fade away like grass, pass—and
will return no more! A picture had somehow
come into his hands, representing a burning
candle, which the winds, with puffed-out
cheeks, were blowing upon from all sides;
below was the inscription: 'Such is the life of
man.' He was very fond of this picture; he
had hung it up in his own room, but at ordinary, not melancholy, times he used to keep
it turned face to the wall, so that it might not
depress him. Harlov, that colossus, was afraid
of death! To the consolations of religion, to
prayer, however, he rarely had recourse in his
fits of melancholy. Even then he chiefly
relied on his own intelligence. He had no
particular religious feeling; he was not often
seen in church; he used to say, it is true, that
he did not go on the ground that, owing to his
corporeal dimensions, he was afraid of squeez-
ing other people out. The fit of depression
commonly ended in Martin Petrovitch's beginning to whistle, and suddenly, in a voice of
thunder, ordering out his droshky, and dashing
off about the neighbourhood, vigorously bran-
dishing his disengaged hand over the peak of
his cap, as though he would say, 'For all that, I
don't care a straw!' He was a regular Russian.

V

STRONG men, like Martin Petrovitch, are for the most part of a phlegmatic disposition ; but he, on the contrary, was rather easily irritated. He was specially short-tempered with a certain Bitchkov, who had found a refuge in our house, where he occupied a position between that of a buffoon and a dependant. He was the brother of Harlov's deceased wife, had been nicknamed Souvenir as a little boy, and Souvenir he had remained for every one, even the servants, who addressed him, it is true, as Souvenir Timofeitch. His real name he seemed hardly to know himself. He was a pitiful creature, looked down upon by every one ; a toady, in fact. He had no teeth on one side of his mouth, which gave his little wrinkled face a crooked appearance. He was in a perpetual fuss and fidget ; he used to poke himself into the maids' room, or into the counting-house, or into the priest's quarters, or else into the bailiff's hut. He was repelled from everywhere, but he only shrugged himself up, and screwed up his little eyes, and laughed a pitiful mawkish laugh, like the sound of rinsing a bottle. It always seemed to me that had Souvenir had money, he would have turned into the basest person, unprincipled, spiteful, even cruel. Poverty kept him within bounds. He was only allowed drink on holidays. He was decently dressed, by my mother's orders, since in the evenings he took a hand in her game of picquet or boston. Souvenir was constantly repeating, 'Certainly, d'rectly, d'rectly.' 'D'rectly what?' my mother would ask, with annoyance. He instantly drew back his hands, in a scare, and lisped, 'At your service, ma'am!' Listening at doors, backbiting, and, above all, quizzing, teasing, were his sole interest, and he used to quiz as though he had a right to, as though he were avenging himself for something. He used to call Martin Petrovitch brother, and tormented him beyond endurance. 'What made you kill my sister, Margarita Timofeevna?' he used to persist, wriggling about before him and sniggering. One day Martin Petrovitch was sitting in the billiard-room, a cool apartment, in which no one had ever seen a single fly, and which our neighbour, disliking heat and sunshine, greatly favoured on this account. He was sitting between the wall and the billiard-table. Souvenir was fidgeting before his bulky person, mocking him, grimacing. . . . Martin Petrovitch wanted to get rid of him, and thrust both hands out in front of him. Luckily for Souvenir he managed to get away, his brother-in-law's open hands came into collision with the edge of the billiard-table, and the billiard-board went flying off all its six screws. . . . . What a mass of batter Souvenir would have been turned into under those mighty hands!

VI

I HAD long been curious to see how Martin
Petrovitch arranged his household, what sort
of a home he had. One day I invited myself
to accompany him on horseback as far as
Eskovo (that was the name of his estate).
'Upon my word, you want to have a look at
my dominion,' was Martin Petrovitch's comment. 'By all means! I'll show you the
garden, and the house, and the threshing-floor,
and everything. I have plenty of everything.'
We set off. It was reckoned hardly more
than a couple of miles from our place to
Eskovo. 'Here it is—my dominion!' Martin
Petrovitch roared suddenly, trying to turn his
immovable neck, and waving his arm to right
and left. 'It's all mine!' Harlov's homestead lay on the top of a sloping hill. At the
bottom, a few wretched-looking peasants' huts
clustered close to a small pond. At the pond,
on a washing platform, an old peasant woman
in a check petticoat was beating some soaked
linen with a bat.

'Axinia!' boomed Martin Petrovitch, but in

such a note that the rooks flew up in a flock from an oat-field near. . . . 'Washing your husband's breeches?'

The peasant woman turned at once and bowed very low.

'Yes, sir,' sounded her weak voice.

' Ay, ay! Yonder, look,' Martin Petrovitch continued, proceeding at a trot alongside a half-rotting wattle fence, 'that is my hemp-patch; and that yonder's the peasants'; see the difference? And this here is my garden; the apple-trees I planted, and the willows I planted too. Else there was no timber of any sort here. Look at that, and learn a lesson!'

We turned into the courtyard, shut in by a fence; right opposite the gate, rose an old tumbledown lodge, with a thatch roof, and steps up to it, raised on posts. On one side stood another, rather newer, and with a tiny attic; but it too was a ramshackly affair. 'Here you may learn a lesson again,' observed Harlov; 'see what a little manor-house our fathers lived in; but now see what a mansion I have built myself.' This 'mansion' was like a house of cards. Five or six dogs, one more ragged and hideous than another, welcomed us with barking. 'Sheep-dogs!' observed Martin Petrovitch. 'Pure-bred Crimeans! Sh, damned brutes! I'll come and strangle you one after another!' On the steps of the new building, there came out a young man, in a long full

nankeen overall, the husband of Martin Petrovitch's elder daughter. Skipping quickly up
to the droshky, he respectfully supported his
father-in-law under the elbow as he got up,
and even made as though he would hold the
gigantic feet, which the latter, bending his
bulky person forward, lifted with a sweeping
movement across the seat ; then he assisted
me to dismount from my horse.

'Anna !' cried Harlov, 'Natalia Nikolaevna's
son has come to pay us a visit ; you must find
some good cheer for him. But where's Evlampia ? ' (Anna was the name of the elder
daughter, Evlampia of the younger.)

'She's not at home ; she's gone into the
fields to get cornflowers,' responded Anna,
appearing at a little window near the door.

'Is there any junket ? ' queried Harlov.

'Yes.'

'And cream too ? '

'Yes.'

'Well, set them on the table, and I'll show
the young gentleman my own room meanwhile.
This way, please, this way,' he added, addressing me, and beckoning with his forefinger. In
his own house he treated me less familiarly ;
as a host he felt obliged to be more formally
respectful. He led me along a corridor. 'Here
is where I abide,' he observed, stepping sideways over the threshold of a wide doorway,
'this is my room. Pray walk in !'

His room turned out to be a big unplastered apartment, almost empty ; on the walls, on nails driven in askew, hung two riding-whips, a three-cornered hat, reddish with wear, a single-barrelled gun, a sabre, a sort of curious horse-collar inlaid with metal plates, and the picture representing a burning candle blown on by the winds. In one corner stood a wooden settle covered with a parti-coloured rug. Hundreds of flies swarmed thickly about the ceiling ; yet the room was cool. But there was a very strong smell of that peculiar odour of the forest which always accompanied Martin Petrovitch.

'Well, is it a nice room?' Harlov questioned me.

'Very nice.'

'Look-ye, there hangs my Dutch horse-collar,' Harlov went on, dropping into his familiar tone again. 'A splendid horse-collar! got it by barter off a Jew. Just you look at it!'

'It's a good horse-collar.'

'It's most practical. And just sniff it . . . what leather!' I smelt the horse-collar. It smelt of rancid oil and nothing else.

'Now, be seated,—there on the stool ; make yourself at home,' observed Harlov, while he himself sank on to the settle, and seemed to fall into a doze, shutting his eyes and even beginning to snore. I gazed at him without speaking with ever fresh wonder ; he was a

23

perfect mountain—there was no other word!
Suddenly he started.

'Anna!' he shouted, while his huge stomach
rose and fell like a wave on the sea; 'what are
you about? Look sharp! Didn't you hear
me?'

'Everything's ready, father; come in,' I
heard his daughter's voice.

I inwardly marvelled at the rapidity with
which Martin Petrovitch's behests had been
carried out; and followed him into the drawing-
room, where, on a table covered with a red
cloth with white flowers on it, lunch was already
prepared: junket, cream, wheaten bread, even
powdered sugar and ginger. While I set to
work on the junket, Martin Petrovitch growled
affectionately, 'Eat, my friend, eat, my dear
boy; don't despise our country cheer,' and
sitting down again in a corner, again seemed
to fall into a doze. Before me, perfectly
motionless, with downcast eyes, stood Anna
Martinovna, while I saw through the window
her husband walking my cob up and down the
yard, and rubbing the chain of the snaffle with
his own hands.

VII

MY mother did not like Harlov's elder daughter; she called her a stuck-up thing. Anna Martinovna scarcely ever came to pay us her respects, and behaved with chilly decorum in my mother's presence, though it was by her good offices she had been well educated at a boarding-school, and had been married, and on her wedding-day had received a thousand roubles and a yellow Turkish shawl, the latter, it is true, a trifle the worse for wear. She was a woman of medium height, thin, very brisk and rapid in her movements, with thick fair hair and a handsome dark face, on which the pale-blue narrow eyes showed up in a rather strange but pleasing way. She had a straight thin nose, her lips were thin too, and her chin was like the loop-end of a hair-pin. No one looking at her could fail to think: 'Well, you are a clever creature—and a spiteful one, too!' And for all that, there was something attractive about her too. Even the dark moles, scattered 'like buck-wheat' over her face, suited her and increased the feeling she inspired.

Her hands thrust into her kerchief, she was slily watching me, looking downwards (I was seated, while she was standing). A wicked little smile strayed about her lips and her cheeks and in the shadow of her long eyelashes. 'Ugh, you pampered little fine gentleman!' this smile seemed to express. Every time she drew a breath, her nostrils slightly distended—this, too, was rather strange. But all the same, it seemed to me that were Anna Martinovna to love me, or even to care to kiss me with her thin cruel lips, I should simply bound up to the ceiling with delight. I knew she was very severe and exacting, that the peasant women and girls went in terror of her—but what of that? Anna Martinovna secretly excited my imagination . . . though after all, I was only fifteen then,—and at that age! . . .

Martin Petrovitch roused himself again. 'Anna!' he shouted, 'you ought to strum something on the pianoforte . . . young gentlemen are fond of that.'

I looked round; there was a pitiful semblance of a piano in the room.

'Yes, father,' responded Anna Martinovna. 'Only what am I to play the young gentleman? He won't find it interesting.'

'Why, what did they teach you at your young ladies' seminary?'

'I've forgotten everything — besides, the notes are broken.'

Anna Martinovna's voice was very pleasant, resonant and rather plaintive—like the note of some birds of prey.

'Very well,' said Martin Petrovitch, and he lapsed into dreaminess again. 'Well,' he began once more, 'wouldn't you like, then, to see the threshing-floor, and have a look round? Volodka will escort you.—Hi, Volodka!' he shouted to his son-in-law, who was still pacing up and down the yard with my horse, 'take the young gentleman to the threshing-floor . . . and show him my farming generally. But I must have a nap! So! good-bye!'

He went out and I after him. Anna Martinovna at once set to work rapidly, and, as it were, angrily, clearing the table. In the doorway, I turned and bowed to her. But she seemed not to notice my bow, and only smiled again, more maliciously than before.

I took my horse from Harlov's son-in-law and led him by the bridle. We went together to the threshing-floor, but as we discovered nothing very remarkable about it, and as he could not suppose any great interest in farming in a young lad like me, we returned through the garden to the main road.

VIII

I WAS well acquainted with Harlov's son-in-law.
His name was Vladimir Vassilievitch Sletkin.
He was an orphan, brought up by my mother,
and the son of a petty official, to whom she
had intrusted some business. He had first
been placed in the district school, then he had
entered the 'seignorial counting-house,' then he
had been put into the service of the government stores, and, finally, married to the daughter
of Martin Petrovitch. My mother used to call
him a little Jew, and certainly, with his curly
hair, his black eyes always moist, like damson
jam, his hook nose, and wide red mouth, he
did suggest the Jewish type. But the colour
of his skin was white and he was altogether
very good-looking. He was of a most obliging
temper, so long as his personal advantage was
not involved. Then he promptly lost all self-
control from greediness, and was moved even
to tears. He was ready to whine the whole
day long to gain the paltriest trifle ; he would
remind one a hundred times over of a promise,
and be hurt and complain if it were not carried

out at once. He liked sauntering about the fields with a gun; and when he happened to get a hare or a wild duck, he would thrust his booty into his game-bag with peculiar zest, saying, 'Now, you may be as tricky as you like, you won't escape me! Now you're *mine*!'

'You've a good horse,' he began in his lisping voice, as he assisted me to get into the saddle; 'I ought to have a horse like that! But where can I get one? I've no such luck. If you'd ask your mamma, now—remind her.'

'Why, has she promised you one?'

'Promised? No; but I thought that in her great kindness——'

'You should apply to Martin Petrovitch.'

'To Martin Petrovitch?' Sletkin repeated, dwelling on each syllable. 'To him I'm no better than a worthless page, like Maximka. He keeps a tight hand on us, that he does, and you get nothing from him for all your toil.'

'Really?'

'Yes, by God. He'll say, "My word's sacred!"—and there, it's as though he's chopped it off with an axe. You may beg or not, it's all one. Besides, Anna Martinovna, my wife, is not in such favour with him as Evlampia Martinovna. O merciful God, bless us and save us!' he suddenly interrupted himself, flinging up his hands in despair. 'Look! what's that? A whole half-rood of oats, our oats, some wretch has gone and cut. The villain! Just see! Thieves! thieves! It's a true saying, to be sure, don't trust Eskovo, Beskovo, Erino, and Byelino! (these were the names of four villages near). Ah, ah, what a thing! A rouble and a half's worth, or, maybe, two roubles, loss!'

In Sletkin's voice, one could almost hear sobs. I gave my horse a poke in the ribs and rode away from him.

Sletkin's ejaculations still reached my hearing, when suddenly at a turn in the road, I came upon the second daughter of Harlov, Evlampia, who had, in the words of Anna Martinovna, gone into the fields to get corn-flowers. A thick wreath of those flowers was twined about her head. We exchanged bows in silence. Evlampia, too, was very good-looking; as much so as her sister, though in a different style. She was tall and stoutly built; everything about her was on a large scale: her head, and her feet and hands, and her snow-white teeth, and especially her eyes, prominent, languishing eyes, of the dark blue of glass beads. Everything about her, while still beautiful, had positively a monumental character (she was a true daughter of Martin Petrovitch). She did not, it seemed, know what to do with her massive fair mane, and she had twisted it in three plaits round her head. Her mouth was charming, crimson and fresh as a rose, and as she talked her upper lip was lifted in the middle in a very fascinating way. But there was something wild and almost fierce in the glance of her huge eyes. 'A free bird, wild Cossack breed,' so Martin Petrovitch used to speak of her. I was in awe of her ... This stately beauty reminded one of her father.

I rode on a little farther and heard her singing in a strong, even, rather harsh voice, a regular peasant voice; suddenly she ceased. I looked round and from the crest of the hill saw her standing beside Harlov's son-in-law, facing the rood of oats. The latter was gesticulating and pointing, but she stood without stirring. The sun lighted up her tall figure, and the wreath of cornflowers shone brilliantly blue on her head.

IX

I BELIEVE I have already mentioned that, for this second daughter of Harlov's too, my mother had already prepared a match. This was one of the poorest of our neighbours, a retired army major, Gavrila Fedulitch Zhitkov, a man no longer young, and, as he himself expressed it, not without a certain complacency, however, as though recommending himself, 'battered and broken down.' He could barely read and write, and was exceedingly stupid, but secretly aspired to become my mother's steward, as he felt himself to be a 'man of action.' 'I can warm the peasant's hides for them, if I can do anything,' he used to say, almost gnashing his own teeth, 'because I was used to it,' he used to explain, 'in my former duties, I mean.' Had Zhitkov been less of a fool, he would have realised that he had not the slightest chance of being steward to my mother, seeing that, for that, it would have been necessary to get rid of the present steward, one Kvitsinsky, a very capable Pole of great character, in whom my mother had the fullest confidence. Zhitkov had a long face, like a horse's; it was all overgrown with hair of a dusty whitish colour; his cheeks were covered with it right up to the eyes; and even in the severest frosts, it was sprinkled with an abundant sweat, like drops of dew. At the sight of my mother, he drew himself upright as a post, his head positively quivered with zeal, his huge hands slapped a little against his thighs, and his whole person seemed to express: 'Command!... and I will strive my utmost!' My mother was under no illusion on the score of his abilities, which did not, however, hinder her from taking steps to marry him to Evlampia.

'Only, will you be able to manage her, my good sir?' she asked him one day.

Zhitkov smiled complacently.

'Upon my word, Natalia Nikolaevna! I used to keep a whole regiment in order; they were tame enough in my hands; and what's this? A trumpery business!'

'A regiment's one thing, sir, but a well-bred girl, a wife, is a very different matter,' my mother observed with displeasure.

'Upon my word, ma'am! Natalia Nikolaevna!' Zhitkov cried again, 'that we're quite able to understand. In one word: a young lady, a delicate person!'

'Well!' my mother decided at length, 'Evlampia won't let herself be trampled upon.'

X

ONE day—it was the month of June, and evening was coming on—a servant announced the arrival of Martin Petrovitch. My mother was surprised : we had not seen him for over a week, but he had never visited us so late before. 'Something has happened!' she exclaimed in an undertone. The face of Martin Petrovitch, when he rolled into the room and at once sank into a chair near the door, wore such an unusual expression, it was so preoccupied and positively pale, that my mother involuntarily repeated her exclamation aloud. Martin Petrovitch fixed his little eyes upon her, was silent for a space, sighed heavily, was silent again, and articulated at last that he had come about something . . . which . . . was of a kind, that on account of . . .

Muttering these disconnected words, he suddenly got up and went out.

My mother rang, ordered the footman, who appeared, to overtake Martin Petrovitch at once and bring him back without fail, but the latter had already had time to get into his droshky and drive away.

Next morning my mother, who was aston-ished and even alarmed, as much by Martin Petrovitch's strange behaviour as by the extra-ordinary expression of his face, was on the point of sending a special messenger to him, when he made his appearance. This time he seemed more composed.

'Tell me, my good friend, tell me,' cried my mother, directly she saw him, 'what ever has happened to you? I thought yesterday, upon my word I did. . . . "Mercy on us!" I thought, "Hasn't our old friend gone right off his head?"'

'I've not gone off my head, madam,' answered Martin Petrovitch; 'I'm not that sort of man. But I want to consult with you.'

'What about?'

'I'm only in doubt, whether it will be agree-able to you in this same contingency——'

'Speak away, speak away, my good sir, but more simply. Don't alarm me! What's this same contingency? Speak more plainly. Or is it your melancholy come upon you again?'

Harlov scowled. 'No, it's not melancholy—that comes upon me in the new moon; but allow me to ask you, madam, what do you think about death?'

My mother was taken aback. 'About what?'

'About death. Can death spare any one whatever in this world?'

'What have you got in your head, my good

friend? Who of us is immortal? For all you 're born a giant, even to you there 'll be an end in time.'

'There will! oh, there will!' Harlov assented and he looked downcast. 'I 've had a vision come to me in my dreams,' he brought out at last.

'What are you saying?' my mother interrupted him.

'A vision in my dreams,' he repeated—'I 'm a seer of visions, you know!'

'You!'

'I. Didn't you know it?' Harlov sighed. 'Well, so. . . . Over a week ago, madam, I lay down, on the very last day of eating meat before St. Peter's fast-day; I lay down after dinner to rest a bit, well, and so I fell asleep, and dreamed a raven colt ran into the room to me. And this colt began sporting about and grinning. Black as a beetle was the raven colt.' Harlov ceased.

'Well?' said my mother.

'And all of a sudden this same colt turns round, and gives me a kick in the left elbow, right in the funny bone. . . . I waked up; my arm would not move nor my leg either. Well, thinks I, it 's paralysis; however, I worked them up and down, and got them to move again; only there were shooting pains in the joints a long time, and there are still. When I open my hand, the pains shoot through the joints.'

36

'Why, Martin Petrovitch, you must have lain upon your arm somehow and crushed it.'

'No, madam; pray, don't talk like that! It was an intimation . . . referring to my death, I mean.'

'Well, upon my word,' my mother was beginning.

'An intimation. Prepare thyself, man, as 'twere to say. And therefore, madam, here is what I have to announce to you, without a moment's delay. Not wishing,' Harlov suddenly began shouting, 'that the same death should come upon me, the servant of God, unawares, I have planned in my own mind this: to divide—now during my lifetime—my estate between my two daughters, Anna and Evlampia, according as God Almighty directs me—' Martin Petrovitch stopped, groaned, and added, 'without a moment's delay.'

'Well, that would be a good idea,' observed my mother; 'though I think you have no need to be in a hurry.'

'And seeing that herein I desire,' Harlov continued, raising his voice still higher, 'to be observant of all due order and legality, so I humbly beg your young son, Dmitri Semyonovitch—I would not venture, madam, to trouble you—I beg the said Dmitri Semyonovitch, your son, and I claim of my kinsman, Bitchkov, as a plain duty, to assist at the ratification of the formal act and transference of possession to my two daughters—Anna, married, and Evlampia, spinster. Which act will be drawn up in readiness the day after to-morrow at twelve o'clock, at my own place, Eskovo, also called Kozulkino, in the presence of the ruling authorities and functionaries, who are thereto invited.'

Martin Petrovitch with difficulty reached the end of this speech, which he had obviously learnt by heart, and which was interspersed with frequent sighs. . . . He seemed to have no breath left in his chest; his pale face was crimson again, and he several times wiped the sweat off it.

'So you've already composed the deed dividing your property?' my mother queried. 'When did you manage that?'

'I managed it . . . oh! Neither eating, nor drinking ——'

'Did you write it yourself?'

'Volodka . . . oh! helped.'

'And have you forwarded a petition?'

'I have, and the chamber has sanctioned it, and notice has been given to the district court, and the temporary division of the local court has . . . oh! . . . been notified to be present.'

My mother laughed. 'I see, Martin Petrovitch, you've made every arrangement already —and how quickly. You've not spared money, I should say?'

'No, indeed, madam.'

'Well, well And you say you want to consult with me. Well, my little Dmitri can go ; and I'll send Souvenir with him, and speak to Kvitsinsky. . . . But you haven't invited Gavrila Fedulitch ? '

'Gavrila Fedulitch—Mr. Zhitkov—has had notice . . . from me also. As a betrothed, it was only fitting.'

Martin Petrovitch had obviously exhausted all the resources of his eloquence. Besides, it always seemed to me that he did not look altogether favourably on the match my mother had made for his daughter ; possibly, he had expected a more advantageous marriage for his darling Evlampia.

He got up from his chair, and made a scrape with his foot. 'Thank you for your consent.'

'Where are you off to?' asked my mother. 'Stay a bit ; I'll order some lunch to be served you.'

'Much obliged,' responded Harlov. 'But I cannot. . . . Oh! I must get home.'

He backed and was about to move sideways, as his habit was, through the door.

'Stop, stop a minute,' my mother went on. 'can you possibly mean to make over the whole of your property without reserve to your daughters?'

'Certainly, without reserve.'

'Well, but how about yourself—where are you going to live?'

Harlov positively flung up his hands in

amazement. 'You ask where? In my house, at home, as I 've lived hitherto . . . so henceforward. Whatever difference could there be?'

'You have such confidence in your daughters and your son-in-law, then?'

'Were you pleased to speak of Volodka? A poor stick like him? Why, I can do as I like with him, whatever it is . . . what authority has he? As for them, my daughters, that is, to care for me till I 'm in the grave, to give me meat and drink, and clothe me. . . . Merciful heavens! it 's their first duty. I shall not long be an eyesore to them. Death 's not over the hills—it 's upon my shoulders.'

'Death is in God's hands,' observed my mother; 'though that is their duty, to be sure. Only pardon me, Martin Petrovitch; your elder girl, Anna, is well known to be proud and imperious, and—well—the second has a fierce look. . . .'

'Natalia Nikolaevna!' Harlov broke in, 'why do you say that? . . . Why, as though they . . . My daughters . . . Why, as though I . . . Forget their duty? Never in their wildest dreams . . . Offer opposition? To whom? Their parent . . . Dare to do such a thing? Have they not my curse to fear? They 've passed their life long in fear and in submission—and all of a sudden . . . Good Lord!'

Harlov choked, there was a rattle in his throat.

'Very well, very well,' my mother made haste to soothe him ; 'only I don't understand all the same what has put it into your head to divide the property up now. It would have come to them afterwards, in any case. I imagine it's your melancholy that's at the bottom of it all.'

'Eh, ma'am,' Harlov rejoined, not without vexation, 'you will keep coming back to that. There is, maybe, a higher power at work in this, and you talk of melancholy. I thought to do this, madam, because in my own person, while still in life, I wish to decide in my presence, who is to possess what, and with what I will reward each, so that they may possess, and feel thankfulness, and carry out my wishes, and what their father and benefactor has resolved upon, they may accept as a bountiful gift.'

Harlov's voice broke again.

'Come, that's enough, that's enough, my good friend,' my mother cut him short ; 'or your raven colt will be putting in an appearance in earnest.'

'O Natalia Nikolaevna, don't talk to me of it,' groaned Harlov. 'That's my death come after me. Forgive my intrusion. And you, my little sir, I shall have the honour of expecting you the day after to-morrow.'

Martin Petrovitch went out ; my mother looked after him, and shook her head significantly.   This is a bad business,' she murmured, 'a bad business.   You noticed'—she addressed herself to me—'he talked, and all the while seemed blinking, as though the sun were in his eyes; that's a bad sign.   When a man's like that, his heart's sure to be heavy, and misfortune threatens him.   You must go over the day after to-morrow with Vikenty Osipovitch and Souvenir.'

ON the day appointed, our big family coach, with seats for four, harnessed with six bay horses, and with the head coachman, the grey-bearded and portly Alexeitch, on the box, rolled smoothly up to the steps of our house. The importance of the act upon which Harlov was about to enter, and the solemnity with which he had invited us, had had their effect on my mother. She had herself given orders for this extraordinary state equipage to be brought out, and had directed Souvenir and me to put on our best clothes. She obviously wished to show respect to her protégé. As for Kvitsinsky, he always wore a frockcoat and white tie. Souvenir chattered like a magpie all the way, giggled, wondered whether his brother would apportion him anything, and thereupon called him a dummy and an old fogey. Kvitsinsky, a man of severe and bilious temperament, could not put up with it at last. 'What can induce you,' he observed, in his distinct Polish accent, 'to keep up such a continual unseemly chatter? Can you really be incapable of sitting quiet without these "wholly superfluous" (his favourite phrase) inanities?' 'All right, d'rectly,' Souvenir muttered discontentedly, and he fixed his squinting eyes on the carriage window. A quarter of an hour had not passed, the smoothly trotting horses had scarcely begun to get warm under the straps of their new harness, when Harlov's homestead came into sight. Through the widely open gate, our coach rolled into the yard. The diminutive postillion, whose legs hardly reached halfway down his horses' body, for the last time leaped up with a babyish shriek into the soft saddle, old Alexeitch at once spread out and raised his elbows, a slight 'wo-o' was heard, and we stopped. The dogs did not bark to greet us, and the serf boys, in long smocks that gaped open over their big stomachs, had all hidden themselves. Harlov's son-in-law was awaiting us in the doorway. I remember I was particularly struck by the birch boughs stuck in on both sides of the steps, as though it were Trinity Sunday. 'Grandeur upon grandeur,' Souvenir, who was the first to alight, squeaked through his nose. And certainly there was a solemn air about everything. Harlov's son-in-law was wearing a plush cravat with a satin bow, and an extraordinarily tight tail-coat; while Maximka, who popped out behind his back, had his hair so saturated with kvas, that it positively dripped. We went into the parlour, and saw Martin

Petrovitch towering—yes, positively towering —motionless, in the middle of the room. I don't know what Souvenir's and Kvitsinsky's feelings were at the sight of his colossal figure; but I felt something akin to awe. Martin Petrovitch was attired in a grey Cossack coat —his militia uniform of 1812 it must have been—with a black stand-up collar. A bronze medal was to be seen on his breast, a sabre hung at his side; he laid his left hand on the hilt, with his right he was leaning on the table, which was covered with a red cloth. Two sheets of paper, full of writing, lay on the table. Harlov stood motionless, not even gasping; and what dignity was expressed in his attitude, what confidence in himself, in his unlimited and unquestionable power! He barely greeted us with a motion of the head, and barely articulating 'Be seated!' pointed the forefinger of his left hand in the direction of some chairs set in a row. Against the right-hand wall of the parlour were standing Harlov's daughters wearing their Sunday clothes: Anna, in a shot lilac-green dress, with a yellow silk sash; Evlampia, in pink, with crimson ribbons. Near them stood Zhitkov, in a new uniform, with the habitual expression of dull and greedy expectation in his eyes, and with a greater profusion of sweat than usual over his hirsute countenance. On the left side of the room sat the priest, in a threadbare snuff-coloured cassock, an old man, with rough brown hair. This head of hair, and the dejected lack-lustre eyes, and the big wrinkled hands, which seemed a burden even to himself, and lay like two rocks on his knees, and the tarred boots which peeped out beneath his cassock, all seemed to tell of a joyless laborious life. His parish was a very poor one. Beside him was the local police captain, a fattish, palish, dirty-looking little gentleman, with soft puffy little hands and feet, black eyes, black short-clipped moustaches, a continual cheerful but yet sickly little smile on his face. He had the reputation of being a great taker of bribes, and even a tyrant, as the expression was in those days. But not only the gentry, even the peasants were used to him, and liked him. He bent very free and easy and rather ironical looks around him ; it was clear that all this 'procedure' amused him. In reality, the only part that had any interest for him was the light lunch and spirits in store for us. But the attorney sitting near him, a lean man with a long face, narrow whiskers from his ears to his nose, as they were worn in the days of Alexander the First, was absorbed with his whole soul in Martin Petrovitch's proceedings, and never took his big serious eyes off him. In his con-centrated attention and sympathy, he kept moving and twisting his lips, though without opening his mouth. Souvenir stationed himself next him, and began talking to him in a whisper, after first informing me that he was the chief freemason in the province. The temporary division of the local court consists, as every one knows, of the police captain, the attorney, and the rural police commissioner; but the latter was either absent or kept himself in the background, so that I did not notice him. He bore, however, the nickname 'the non-existent' among us in the district, just as there are tramps called 'the non-identified.' I sat next Souvenir, Kvitsinsky next me. The face of the practical Pole showed unmistakeable annoyance at our 'wholly superfluous' expedition, and unnecessary waste of time. . . . 'A grand lady's caprices! these Russian grandees' fancies!' he seemed to be murmuring to himself. . . . 'Ugh, these Russians!'

XII

WHEN we were all seated, Martin Petrovitch hunched his shoulders, cleared his throat, scanned us all with his bear-like little eyes, and with a noisy sigh began as follows :

'Gentlemen, I have called you together for the following purpose. I am grown old, gentlemen, and overcome by infirmities. . . . Already I have had an intimation, the hour of death steals on, like a thief in the night. . . . Isn't that so, father?' he addressed the priest.

The priest started. 'Quite so, quite so,' he mumbled, his beard shaking.

'And therefore,' continued Martin Petrovitch, suddenly raising his voice, 'not wishing the said death to come upon me unawares, I purposed' . . . Martin Petrovitch proceeded to repeat, word for word, the speech he had made to my mother two days before. 'In accordance with this my determination,' he shouted louder than ever, 'this deed' (he struck his hand on the papers lying on the table) 'has been drawn up by me, and the presiding authorities have been invited by me, and wherein my will consists the following points will treat. I have ruled, my day is over!'

Martin Petrovitch put his round iron spectacles on his nose, took one of the written sheets from the table, and began:

'Deed of partition of the estate of the retired non-commissioned officer and nobleman, Martin Harlov, drawn up by himself in his full and right understanding, and by his own good judgment, and wherein is precisely defined what benefits are assigned to his two daughters, Anna and Evlampia—bow!'—(they bowed), 'and in what way the serfs and other property, and live stock, be apportioned between the said daughters! Under my hand!'

'This is their document!' the police captain whispered to Kvitsinsky, with his invariable smile, 'they want to read it for the beauty of the style, but the legal deed is made out formally, without all these flourishes.'

Souvenir was beginning to snigger. . . .

'In accordance with my will,' put in Harlov, who had caught the police captain's remark.

'In accordance in every point,' the latter hastened to respond cheerfully; 'only, as you're aware, Martin Petrovitch, there's no dispensing with formality. And unnecessary details have been removed. For the chamber can't enter into the question of spotted cows and fancy drakes.'

'Come here!' boomed Harlov to his son-in-law, who had come into the room behind us, and remained standing with an obsequious air near the door. He skipped up to his father-in-law at once.

'There, take it and read! It's hard for me. Only mind and don't mumble it! Let all the gentlemen present be able to understand it.'

Sletkin took the paper in both hands, and began timidly, but distinctly, and with taste and feeling, to read the deed of partition. There was set forth in it with the greatest accuracy just what was assigned to Anna and what to Evlampia, and how the division was to be made. Harlov from time to time interspersed the reading with phrases. 'Do you hear, that's for you, Anna, for your zeal!' or, 'That I give you, Evlampia!' and both the sisters bowed, Anna from the waist, Evlampia simply with a motion of the head. Harlov looked at them with stern dignity. 'The farm house' (the little new building) was assigned by him to Evlampia, as the younger daughter, 'by the well-known custom.' The reader's voice quivered and resounded at these words, unfavourable for himself; while Zhitkov licked his lips. Evlampia gave him a sidelong glance; had I been in Zhitkov's shoes, I should not have liked that glance. The scornful expression, characteristic of Evlampia, as of every genuine Russian beauty, had a peculiar shade at that

moment. For himself, Martin Petrovitch
reserved the right to go on living in the rooms
he occupied, and assigned to himself, under
the name of 'rations,' a full allowance 'of
normal provisions,' and ten roubles a month
for clothes. The last phrase of the deed
Harlov wished to read himself. 'And this
my parental will,' it ran, 'to carry out and
observe is a sacred and binding duty on my
daughters, seeing it is a command ; seeing
that I am, after God, their father and head,
and am not bounden to render an account to
any, nor have so rendered. And do they carry
out my will, so will my fatherly blessing be
with them, but should they not so do, which
God forbid, then will they be overtaken by my
paternal curse that cannot be averted, now and
for ever, amen !' Harlov raised the deed high
above his head. Anna at once dropped on her
knees and touched the ground with her forehead ; her husband, too, doubled up after her.
'Well, and you?' Harlov turned to Evlampia.
She crimsoned all over, and she too bowed to
the earth ; Zhitkov bent his whole carcase
forward.

'Sign !' cried Harlov, pointing his forefinger
to the bottom of the deed. 'Here : "I thank
and accept, Anna. I thank and accept, Evlampia !"'

Both daughters rose. and signed one after
another. Sletkin rose too, and was feeling

after the pen, but Harlov moved him aside, sticking his middle finger into his cravat, so that he gasped. The silence lasted a moment. Suddenly Martin Petrovitch gave a sort of sob, and muttering, 'Well, now it's all yours!' moved away. His daughters and son-in-law looked at one another, went up to him and began kissing him just above his elbow. His shoulder they could not reach.

XIII

THE police captain read the real formal document, the deed of gift, drawn up by Martin Petrovitch. Then he went out on to the steps with the attorney and explained what had taken place to the crowd assembled at the gates, consisting of the witnesses required by law and other people from the neighbourhood, Harlov's peasants, and a few house-serfs. Then began the ceremony of the new owners entering into possession. They came out, too, upon the steps, and the police captain pointed to them when, slightly scowling with one eyebrow, while his careless face assumed for an instant a threatening air, he exhorted the crowd to 'subordination.' He might well have dispensed with these exhortations: a less unruly set of countenances than those of the Harlov peasants, I imagine, have never existed in creation. Clothed in thin smocks and torn sheepskins, but very tightly girt round their waists, as is always the peasants' way on solemn occasions, they stood motionless as though cut out of stone, and whenever the police captain uttered

53

any exclamation such as, 'D'ye hear, you
brutes? d'ye understand, you devils?' they
suddenly bowed all at once, as though at the
word of command. Each of these 'brutes and
devils' held his cap tight in both hands, and
never took his eyes off the window, where
Martin Petrovitch's figure was visible. The
witnesses themselves were hardly less awed.
'Is any impediment known to you,' the police
captain roared at them, 'against the entrance
into possession of these the sole and legitimate
heirs and daughters of Martin Petrovitch
Harlov?'

All the witnesses seemed to huddle together
at once.

'Do you know any, you devils?' the police
captain shouted again.

'We know nothing, your excellency,' responded sturdily a little old man, marked with
small-pox, with a clipped beard and whiskers,
an old soldier.

'I say! Eremeitch's a bold fellow!' the
witnesses said of him as they dispersed.

In spite of the police captain's entreaties,
Harlov would not come out with his daughters
on to the steps. 'My subjects will obey my
will without that!' he answered. Something
like sadness had come over him on the completion of the conveyance. His face had grown
pale. This new unprecedented expression of
sadness looked so out of place on Martin

Petrovitch's broad and kindly features that I positively was at a loss what to think. Was an attack of melancholy coming over him? The peasants, on their side, too, were obviously puzzled. And no wonder! 'The master's alive,—there he stands, and such a master, too; Martin Petrovitch! And all of a sudden he won't be their owner. . . . A queer thing!' I don't know whether Harlov had an inkling of the notions that were straying through his 'subjects'' heads, or whether he wanted to display his power for the last time, but he suddenly opened the little window, stuck his head out, and shouted in a voice of thunder, 'obedience!' Then he slammed-to the window. The peasants' bewilderment was certainly not dispelled nor decreased by this proceeding. They became stonier than ever, and even seemed to cease looking at anything. The group of house-serfs (among them were two sturdy wenches, in short chintz gowns, with muscles such as one might perhaps match in Michael Angelo's 'Last Judgment,' and one utterly decrepit old man, hoary with age and half blind, in a threadbare frieze cloak, rumoured to have been 'cornet-player' in the days of Potemkin,—the page Maximka, Harlov had reserved for himself) this group showed more life than the peasants; at least, it moved restlessly about. The new mistresses themselves were very dignified in their attitude, especially

Anna. Her thin lips tightly compressed, she looked obstinately down . . . her stern figure augured little good to the house-serfs. Evlampia, too, did not raise her eyes; only once she turned round and deliberately, as it were with surprise, scanned her betrothed, Zhitkov, who had thought fit, following Sletkin, to come out, too, on to the steps. 'What business have you here?' those handsome prominent eyes seemed to demand. Sletkin was the most changed of all. A bustling cheeriness showed itself in his whole bearing, as though he were overtaken by hunger; the movements of his head and his legs were as obsequious as ever but how gleefully he kept working his arms, how fussily he twitched his shoulder-blades. 'Arrived at last!' he seemed to say. Having finished the ceremony of the entrance into possession, the police captain, whose mouth was literally watering at the prospect of lunch, rubbed his hands in that peculiar manner which usually precedes the tossing-off of the first glass of spirits. But it appeared that Martin Petrovitch wished first to have a service performed with sprinklings of holy water. The priest put on an ancient and decrepit chasuble; a decrepit deacon came out of the kitchen, with difficulty kindling the incense in an old brazen church-vessel. The service began. Harlov sighed continually; he was unable, owing to his corpulence, to bow to the ground,

but crossing himself with his right hand and
bending his head, he pointed with the forefinger of his left hand to the floor. Sletkin
positively beamed and even shed tears. Zhitkov, with dignity, in martial fashion, flourished
his fingers only slightly between the third and
fourth button of his uniform. Kvitsinsky, as
a Catholic, remained in the next room. But
the attorney prayed so fervently, sighed so
sympathetically after Martin Petrovitch, and
so persistently muttered and chewed his lips,
turning his eyes upwards, that I felt moved, as
I looked at him, and began to pray fervently
too. At the conclusion of the service and the
sprinkling with holy water, during which every
one present, even the blind cornet-player, the
contemporary of Potemkin, even Kvitsinsky,
moistened their eyes with holy water, Anna and
Evlampia once more, at Martin Petrovitch's
bidding, prostrated themselves to the ground to
thank him. Then at last came the moment of
lunch. There were a great many dishes and all
very nice; we all ate terribly much. The inevitable bottle of Don wine made its appearance.
The police captain, who was of all of us the
most familiar with the usages of the world, and
besides, the representative of government, was
the first to propose the toast to the health 'of
the fair proprietresses!' Then he proposed we
should drink to the health of our most honoured
and most generous-hearted friend, Martin

Petrovitch. At the words 'most generous-hearted,' Sletkin uttered a shrill little cry and ran to kiss his benefactor. . . . 'There, that'll do, that'll do,' muttered Harlov, as it were with annoyance, keeping him off with his elbow . . . But at this point a not quite pleasant, as they say, incident took place.

XIV

Souvenir, who had been drinking continuously ever since the beginning of luncheon, suddenly got up from his chair as red as a beetroot, and pointing his finger at Martin Petrovitch, went off into his mawkish, paltry laugh.

'Generous-hearted! Generous-hearted!' he began croaking; 'but we shall see whether this generosity will be much to his taste when he's stripped naked, the servant of God . . . and out in the snow, too!'

'What rot are you talking, fool?' said Harlov contemptuously.

'Fool! fool!' repeated Souvenir. 'God Almighty alone knows which of us is the real fool. But you, brother, did my sister, your wife, to her death, and now you've done for yourself . . . ha-ha-ha!'

'How dare you insult our honoured bene-factor?' Sletkin began shrilly, and, tearing himself away from Martin Petrovitch, whose shoulder he had clutched, he flew at Souvenir. 'But let me tell you, if our benefactor desires it, we can cancel the deed this very minute!'

'And yet, you'll strip him naked, and turn him out into the snow . . .' returned Souvenir, retreating behind Kvitsinsky.

'Silence!' thundered Harlov. 'I'll pound you into a jelly! And you hold your tongue too, puppy!' he turned to Sletkin; 'don't put in your word where you're not wanted! If I, Martin Petrovitch Harlov, have decided to make a deed of partition, who can cancel the same act against my will? Why, in the whole world there is no power.' . . .

'Martin Petrovitch!' the attorney began in a mellow bass—he too had drunk a good deal, but his dignity was only increased thereby— 'but how if the gentleman has spoken the truth? You have done a generous action; to be sure, but how if—God forbid—in reality in place of fitting gratitude, some affront come of it?'

I stole a glance at both Martin Petrovitch's daughters. Anna's eyes were simply pinned upon the speaker, and a face more spiteful, more snake-like, and more beautiful in its very spite I had certainly never seen! Evlampia sat turned away, with her arms folded. A smile more scornful than ever curved her full, rosy lips.

Harlov got up from his chair, opened his mouth, but apparently his tongue failed him. . . . He suddenly brought his fist down on the table, so that everything in the room danced and rang.

'Father,' Anna said hurriedly, 'they do not
know us, and that is why they judge of us so.
But don't, please, make yourself ill. You are
angered for nothing, indeed; see, your face is,
as it were, twisted awry.'

Harlov looked towards Evlampia; she did
not stir, though Zhitkov, sitting beside her,
gave her a poke in the side.

'Thank you, my daughter Anna,' said Harlov
huskily; 'you are a sensible girl; I rely upon
you and on your husband too.' Sletkin once
more gave vent to a shrill little sound; Zhitkov
expanded his chest and gave a little scrape
with his foot; but Harlov did not observe his
efforts. 'This dolt,' he went on, with a motion
of his chin in the direction of Souvenir, 'is
pleased to get a chance to teaze me; but you,
my dear sir,' he addressed himself to the
attorney, 'it is not for you to pass judgment
on Martin Harlov; that is something beyond
you. Though you are a man in official position, your words are most foolish. Besides, the
deed is done, there will be no going back from
my determination. . . . Now, I will wish you
good-day, I am going away. I am no longer
the master of this house, but a guest in it.
Anna, do you do your best; but I will go to
my own room. Enough!'

Martin Petrovitch turned his back on us, and,
without adding another word, walked deliberately out of the room.

This sudden withdrawal on the part of our host could not but break up the party, especially as the two hostesses also vanished not long after. Sletkin vainly tried to keep us. The police captain did not fail to blame the attorney for his uncalled-for candour. 'Couldn't help it!' the latter responded. . . . 'My conscience spoke.'

'There, you see that he's a mason,' Souvenir whispered to me.

'Conscience!' retorted the police captain. 'We know all about your conscience! I suppose it's in your pocket, just the same as it is with us sinners!'

The priest, meanwhile, even though already on his feet, foreseeing the speedy termination of the repast, lifted mouthful after mouthful to his mouth without a pause.

'You've got a fine appetite, I see,' Sletkin observed to him sharply.

'Storing up for the future,' the priest responded with a meek grimace; years of hunger were expressed in that reply.

The carriages rattled up . . . and we separated. On the way home, no one hindered Souvenir's chatter and silly tricks, as Kvitsinsky had announced that he was sick of all this 'wholly superfluous' unpleasantness, and had set off home before us on foot. In his place, Zhitkov took a seat in our coach. The retired major wore a most dissatisfied expression, and kept twitching his moustaches like a spider.

'Well, your noble Excellency,' lisped Souvenir, 'is subordination exploded, eh? Wait a bit and see what will happen! They'll give you the sack too. Ah, a poor bridegroom you are, a poor bridegroom, an unlucky bridegroom!'

Souvenir was positively beside himself; while poor Zhitkov could do nothing but twitch his moustaches.

When I got home I told my mother all I had seen. She heard me to the end, and shook her head several times. 'It's a bad business,' was her comment. 'I don't like all these innovations!'

XV

NEXT day Martin Petrovitch came to dinner. My mother congratulated him on the successful conclusion of his project. 'You are now a free man,' she said, 'and ought to feel more at ease.'

'More at ease, to be sure, madam,' answered Martin Petrovitch, by no means, however, showing in the expression of his face that he really was more at ease. 'Now I can meditate upon my soul, and make ready for my last hour, as I ought.'

'Well,' queried my mother, 'and do the shooting pains still tingle in your arms?'

Harlov twice clenched and unclenched his left arm. 'They do, madam; and I've something else to tell you. As I begin to drop asleep, some one cries in my head, "Take care!" "Take care!"'

'That's nerves,' observed my mother, and she began speaking of the previous day, and referred to certain circumstances which had attended the completion of the deed of partition. . . .

'To be sure, to be sure,' Harlov interrupted

her, 'there was something of the sort . . . of no consequence. Only there's something I would tell you,' he added, hesitating—'I was not disturbed yesterday by Souvenir's silly words— even Mr. Attorney, though he's no fool—even he did not trouble me; no, it was quite another person disturbed me ——' Here Harlov faltered.

'Who?' asked my mother.

Harlov fastened his eyes upon her: 'Evlampia!'

'Evlampia? Your daughter? How was that?'

'Upon my word, madam, she was like a stone! nothing but a statue! Can it be she has no feeling? Her sister, Anna—well, she was all she should be. She's a keen-witted creature! But Evlampia—why, I'd shown her —I must own—so much partiality! Can it be she's no feeling for me! It's clear I'm in a bad way; it's clear I've a feeling that I'm not long for this world, since I make over everything to them; and yet she's like a stone! she might at least utter a sound! Bows—yes, she bows, but there's no thankfulness to be seen.'

'There, give over,' observed my mother, 'we'll marry her to Gavrila Fedulitch . . . she'll soon get softer in his hands.'

Martin Petrovitch once more looked from under his brows at my mother. 'Well, there's

Gavrila Fedulitch, to be sure! You have confidence in him, then, madam?'

'I've confidence in him.'

'Very well; you should know best, to be sure. But Evlampia, let me tell you, is like me. The character is just the same. She has the wild Cossack blood, and her heart's like a burning coal!'

'Why, do you mean to tell me you've a heart like that, my dear sir?'

Harlov made no answer. A brief silence followed.

'What are you going to do, Martin Petrovitch,' my mother began, 'in what way do you mean to set about saving your soul now? Will you set off to Mitrophan or to Kiev, or may be you'll go to the Optin desert, as it's in the neighbourhood? There, they do say, there's a holy monk appeared . . . Father Makary they call him, no one remembers any one like him! He sees right through all sins.'

'If she really turns out an ungrateful daughter,' Harlov enunciated in a husky voice, 'then it would be better for me, I believe, to kill her with my own hands!'

'What are you saying! Lord, have mercy on you!' cried my mother. 'Think what you're saying! There, see, what a pretty pass it's come to. You should have listened to me the other day when you came to consult me! Now, here, you'll go tormenting yourself, instead of

66

thinking of your soul! You'll be tormenting yourself, and all to no purpose! Yes!
Here you're complaining now, and faint-
hearted . . .'

This reproach seemed to stab Harlov to the
heart. All his old pride came back to him
with a rush. He shook himself, and thrust
out his chin. 'I am not a man, madam, Natalia
Nikolaevna, to complain or be faint-hearted,' he
began sullenly. 'I simply wished to reveal my
feelings to you as my benefactress and a person
I respect. But the Lord God knows (here he
raised his hand high above his head) that this
globe of earth may crumble to pieces before I
will go back from my word, or . . . (here he
positively snorted) show a faint heart, or regret
what I have done! I had good reasons, be
sure! My daughters will never forget their
duty, for ever and ever, amen!'

My mother stopped her ears. 'What's this
for, my good sir, like a trumpet-blast! If you
really have such faith in your family, well, praise
the Lord for it! You've quite put my brains
in a whirl!'

Martin Petrovitch begged pardon, sighed
twice, and was silent. My mother once more
referred to Kiev, the Optin desert, and Father
Makary. . . . Harlov assented, said that 'he
must . . . he must . . . he would have to . .
his soul' . . . and that was all. He did not
regain his cheerfulness before he went away.

From time to time he clenched and unclenched his fist, looked at his open hand, said that what he feared above everything was dying without repentance, from a stroke, and that he had made a vow to himself not to get angry, as anger vitiated his blood and drove it to his head. . . . Besides, he had now withdrawn from everything. What grounds could he have for getting angry? Let other people trouble themselves now and vitiate their blood!

As he took leave of my mother he looked at her in a strange way, mournfully and questioningly ... and suddenly, with a rapid movement, drew out of his pocket the volume of *The Worker's Leisure-Hour*, and thrust it into my mother's hand.

'What's that?' she inquired.

'Read . . . here,' he said hurriedly, 'where the corner's turned down, about death. It seems to me, it's terribly well said, but I can't make it out at all. Can't you explain it to me, my benefactress? I'll come back again and you explain it me.'

With these words Martin Petrovitch went away.

'He's in a bad way, he's in a bad way,' observed my mother, directly he had disappeared through the doorway, and she set to work upon the *Leisure-Hour*. On the page turned down by Harlov were the following words:

Death is a grand and solemn work of nature. It is nothing else than that the spirit, inasmuch as it is lighter, finer, and infinitely more penetrating than those elements under whose sway it has been subject, nay, even than the force of electricity itself, so is chemically purified and striveth upward till what time it attaineth an equally spiritual abiding-place for itself . . .' and so on.

My mother read this passage through twice, and exclaiming, 'Pooh!' she flung the book away.

Three days later, she received the news that her sister's husband was dead, and set off to her sister's country-seat, taking me with her. My mother proposed to spend a month with her, but she stayed on till late in the autumn, and it was only at the end of September that we returned to our own estate.

XVI

THE first news with which my valet, Prokofy, greeted me (he regarded himself as the seignorial huntsman) was that there was an immense number of wild snipe on the wing, and that in the birch-copse near Eskovo (Harlov's property), especially, they were simply swarming. I had three hours before me till dinner-time. I promptly seized my gun and my game-bag, and with Prokofy and a setter-dog, hastened to the Eskovo copse. We certainly did find a great many wild snipe there, and, firing about thirty charges, killed five. As I hurried homewards with my booty, I saw a peasant ploughing near the road-side. His horse had stopped, and with tearful and angry abuse he was mercilessly tugging with the cord reins at the animal's head, which was bent on one side. I looked attentively at the luckless beast, whose ribs were all but through its skin, and, bathed in sweat, heaved up and down with convulsive, irregular movements like a blacksmith's bellows. I recognised it at once as the decrepit old mare, with the scar on her

shoulder, who had served Martin Petrovitch
so many years.

'Is Mr. Harlov living?' I asked Prokofy.
The chase had so completely absorbed us, that
up to that instant we had not talked of anything.

'Yes, he's alive. Why?'

'But that's his mare, isn't it? Do you mean
to say he's sold her?'

'His mare it is, to be sure; but as to selling,
he never sold her. But they took her away
from him, and handed her over to that peasant.'

'How, took it? And he consented?'

'They never asked his consent. Things have
changed here in your absence,' Prokofy observed,
with a faint smile in response to my look of
amazement; 'worse luck! My goodness, yes!
Now Sletkin's master, and orders every one
about.'

'But Martin Petrovitch?'

'Why, Martin Petrovitch has become the
very last person here, you may say. He's on
bread and water,—what more can one say?
They've crushed him altogether. Mark my
words; they'll drive him out of the house.'

The idea that it was possible to *drive* such a
giant had never entered my head. 'And what
does Zhitkov say to it?' I asked at last. 'I
suppose he's married to the second daughter?'

'Married?' repeated Prokofy, and this time
he grinned all over his face. 'They won't let

him into the house. "We don't want you," they say; "get along home with you." It's as I said; Sletkin directs every one.'

'But what does the young lady say?'

'Evlampia Martinovna? Ah, master, I could tell you . . . but you're young—one must think of that. Things are going on here that are . . . oh! . . . oh! . . . oh! Hey! why Dianka's setting, I do believe!'

My dog actually had stopped short, before a thick oak bush which bordered a narrow ravine by the roadside. Prokofy and I ran up to the dog; a snipe flew up out of the bush, we both fired at it and missed; the snipe settled in another place; we followed it.

The soup was already on the table when I got back. My mother scolded me. 'What's the meaning of it?' she said with displeasure; 'the very first day, and you keep us waiting for dinner.' I brought her the wild snipe I had killed; she did not even look at them. There were also in the room Souvenir, Kvitsinsky, and Zhitkov. The retired major was huddled in a corner, for all the world like a schoolboy in disgrace. His face wore an expression of mingled confusion and annoyance; his eyes were red . . . One might positively have imagined he had recently been in tears. My mother remained in an ill humour. I was at no great pains to surmise that my late arrival did not count for much in it. During dinner-time she hardly talked at all. The major turned beseeching glances upon her from time to time, but ate a good dinner nevertheless. Souvenir was all of a shake. Kvitsinsky preserved his habitual self-confidence of demeanour.

'Vikenty Ósipitch,' my mother addressed him, ' I beg you to send a carriage to-morrow for Martin Petrovitch, since it has come to my knowledge that he has none of his own. And bid them tell him to come without fail, that I desire to see him.'

Kvitsinsky was about to make some rejoinder, but he restrained himself.

' And let Sletkin know,' continued my mother, ' that I command him to present himself before me . . . Do you hear? I com . . . mand !'

'Yes, just so ، . . that scoundrel ought——' Zhitkov was beginning in a subdued voice; but my mother gave him such a contemptuous look, that he promptly turned away and was silent.

' Do you hear? I command !' repeated my mother.

' Certainly, madam,' Kvitsinsky replied submissively but with dignity.

' Martin Petrovitch won't come !' Souvenir whispered to me, as he came out of the dining-room with me after dinner. ' You should just see what's happened to him ! It's past comprehension ! It's come to this, that whatever

73

they say to him, he doesn't understand a word! Yes! They've got the snake under the pitchfork!'

And Souvenir went off into his revolting laugh.

XVII

SOUVENIR'S prediction turned out correct. Martin Petrovitch would not come to my mother. She was not at all pleased with this, and despatched a letter to him. He sent her a square bit of paper, on which the following words were written in big letters : 'Indeed I can't. I should die of shame. Let me go to my ruin. Thanks. Don't torture me.—Martin Harlov.' Sletkin did come, but not on the day on which my mother had 'commanded' his attendance, but twenty-four hours later. My mother gave orders that he should be shown into her boudoir. . . . God knows what their interview was about, but it did not last long ; a quarter of an hour, not more. Sletkin came out of my mother's room, crimson all over, and with such a viciously spiteful and insolent expression of face, that, meeting him in the drawing-room, I was simply petrified, while Souvenir, who was hanging about there, stopped short in the middle of a snigger. My mother came out of her boudoir, also very red in the

face, and announced, in the hearing of all, that
Mr. Sletkin was never, upon any pretext, to be
admitted to her presence again, and that if
Martin Petrovitch's daughters were to make
bold—they've impudence enough, said she—
to present themselves, they, too, were to be
refused admittance. At dinner-time she suddenly exclaimed, 'The vile little Jew! I picked
him out of the gutter, I made him a career,
he owes everything, everything to me,—and he
dares to tell me I've no business to meddle in
their affairs! that Martin Petrovitch is full of
whims and fancies, and it's impossible to
humour him! Humour him, indeed! What a
thing to say! Ah, he's an ungrateful wretch!
An insolent little Jew!'

Major Zhitkov, who happened to be one of the
company at dinner, imagined that now it was
no less than the will of the Almighty for him to
seize the opportunity and put in his word . . .
but my mother promptly settled him. 'Well,
and you're a fine one, too, my man!' she commented. 'Couldn't get the upper hand of a
girl, and he an officer! In command of a
squadron! I can fancy how it obeyed you!
He take a steward's place indeed! a fine steward
he'd make!'

Kvitsinsky, who was sitting at the end of the
table, smiled to himself a little malignantly,
while poor Zhitkov could do nothing but twitch
his moustaches, lift his eyebrows, and bury

the whole of his hirsute countenance in his napkin.

After dinner, he went out on to the steps to smoke his pipe as usual, and he struck me as so miserable and forlorn, that, although I had never liked him, I joined myself on to him at once.

'How was it, Gavrila Fedulitch,' I began without further beating about the bush, 'that your affair with Evlampia Martinovna was broken off? I'd expected you to be married long ago.'

The retired major looked at me dejectedly.

'A snake in the grass,' he began, uttering each letter of each syllable with bitter distinctness, 'has poisoned me with his fang, and turned all my hopes in life to ashes. And I could tell you, Dmitri Semyonovitch, all his hellish wiles, but I'm afraid of angering your mamma. ('You're young yet'—Prokofy's expression flashed across my mind.) 'Even as it is'——Zhitkov groaned.

'Patience . . . patience . . . nothing else is left me. (He struck his fist upon his chest.) Patience, old soldier, patience. I served the Tsar faithfully . . . honourably . . . yes. I spared neither blood nor sweat, and now see what I am brought to. Had it been in the regiment—and the matter depending upon me,' he continued after a short silence, spent in convulsively sucking at his cherrywood pipe,

'I'd have . . . I'd have given it him with the flat side of my sword . . . three times over . . . till he'd had enough . . .'

Zhitkov took the pipe out of his mouth, and fixed his eyes on vacancy, as though admiring the picture he had conjured up.

Souvenir ran up, and began quizzing the major. I turned away from them, and determined, come what may, I would see Martin Petrovitch with my own eyes. . . . My boyish curiosity was greatly stirred.

XVIII

NEXT day I set out with my gun and dog. but without Prokofy, to the Eskovo copse. It was an exquisite day; I fancy there are no days like that in September anywhere but in Russia. The stillness was such that one could hear, a hundred paces off, the squirrel hopping over the dry leaves, and the broken twig just feebly catching at the other branches, and falling, at last, on the soft grass—to lie there for ever, not to stir again till it rotted away. The air, neither warm nor chill, but only fragrant, and as it were keen, was faintly, deliciously stinging in my eyes and on my cheeks. A long spider-web, delicate as a silken thread, with a white ball in the middle, floated smoothly in the air, and sticking to the butt-end of my gun, stretched straight out in the air—a sign of settled and warm weather. The sun shone with a brightness as soft as moonlight. Wild snipe were to be met with pretty often; but I did not pay special attention to them. I knew that the copse went on almost to Harlov's homestead, right up to the hedge of his garden, and I turned

my steps in that direction, though I could not
even imagine how I should get into the place
itself, and was even doubtful whether I ought to
try to do so, as my mother was so angry with
its new owners. Sounds of life and humanity
reached me from no great distance. I listened.
. . . Some one was coming through the copse . . .
straight towards me.

'You should have said so straight out, dear,'
I heard a woman's voice.

'Be reasonable,' another voice broke in, the
voice of a man. 'Can one do it all at once?'

I knew the voices. There was the gleam of
a woman's blue gown through the reddening
nut bushes. Beside it stood a dark full coat.
Another instant—and there stepped out into
the glade, five paces from me, Sletkin and
Evlampia.

They were disconcerted at once. Evlampia
promptly stepped back, away into the bushes.
Sletkin thought a little, and came up to me.
There was not a trace to be seen in his face of
the obsequious meekness, with which he had
paced up and down Harlov's courtyard, four
months before, rubbing up my horse's snaffle.
But neither could I perceive in it the insolent
defiance, which had so struck me on the previous day, on the threshold of my mother's
boudoir. It was still as white and pretty as
ever, but seemed broader and more solid.

'Well, have you shot many snipe?' he asked

me, raising his cap, smiling, and passing his hand over his black curls; 'you are shooting in our copse. . . . You are very welcome. We would not hinder you. . . . Quite the contrary.'

'I have killed nothing to-day,' I rejoined, answering his first question; 'and I will go out of your copse this instant.'

Sletkin hurriedly put on his cap. 'Indeed, why so? We would not drive you out—indeed, we're delighted. . . . Here's Evlampia Martinovna will say the same. Evlampia Martinovna, come here. Where have you hidden yourself?' Evlampia's head appeared behind the bushes. But she did not come up to us. She had grown prettier, and seemed taller and bigger than ever.

'I'm very glad, to tell the truth,' Sletkin went on, 'that I have met you. Though you are still young in years, you have plenty of good sense already. Your mother was pleased to be very angry with me yesterday—she would not listen to reason of any sort from me, but I declare, as before God, so before you now, I am not to blame in any way. We can't treat Martin Petrovitch otherwise than we do; he's fallen into complete dotage. One can't humour all his whims, really. But we show him all due respect. Only ask Evlampia Martinovna.'

Evlampia did not stir; her habitual scornful smile flickered about her lips, and her large eyes watched us with no friendly expression.

'But why, Vladimir Vassilievitch, have you sold Martin Petrovitch's mare?' (I was particularly impressed by that mare being in the possession of a peasant.)

'His mare, why did we sell it? Why, Lord have mercy on us—what use was she? She was simply eating her head off. But with the peasant she can work at the plough anyway. As for Martin Petrovitch, if he takes a fancy to drive out anywhere, he's only to ask us. We wouldn't refuse him a conveyance. On a holiday, we should be pleased.'

'Vladimir Vassilievitch,' said Evlampia huskily, as though calling him away, and she still did not stir from her place. She was twisting some stalks of ripple grass round her fingers and snapping off their heads, slapping them against each other.

'About the page Maximka again,' Sletkin went on, 'Martin Petrovitch complains because we've taken him away and apprenticed him. But kindly consider the matter for yourself. Why, what had he to do waiting on Martin Petrovitch? Kick up his heels; nothing more. And he couldn't even wait on him properly; on account of his stupidity and his youth. Now we have sent him away to a harness-maker's. He'll be turned into a first-rate handicraftsman—and make a good thing of it for himself—and pay us ransom-money too. And, living in a small way as we do, that's a matter of importance. On a little farm like ours, one can't afford to let anything slip.'

'And this is the man Martin Petrovitch called a "poor stick,"' I thought. 'But who reads to Martin Petrovitch now?' I asked.

'Why, what is there to read? He had one book—but, luckily, that's been mislaid somewhere. . . . And what use is reading at his age.'

'And who shaves him?' I asked again.

Sletkin gave an approving laugh, as though in response to an amusing joke. 'Why, nobody. At first he used to singe his beard in the candle—but now he lets it be altogether. And it's lovely!'

'Vladimir Vassilievitch!' Evlampia repeated insistently: 'Vladimir Vassilievitch!'

Sletkin made her a sign with his hand.

'Martin Petrovitch is clothed and cared for, and eats what we do. What more does he want? He declared himself that he wanted nothing more in this world but to think of his soul. If only he would realise that everything now, however you look at it, is ours. He says too that we don't pay him his allowance. But we've not always got money ourselves; and what does he want with it, when he has everything provided him? And we treat him as one of the family too. I'm telling you the truth. The rooms, for instance, which he occupies—how we need them! there's simply not room to turn round without them; but we don't say

a word—we put up with it. We even think
how to provide amusement for him. There, on
St. Peter's Day, I bought him some excellent
hooks in the town—real English ones, expen-
sive hooks, to catch fish. There are lots of
carp in our pond. Let him sit and fish; in an
hour or two, there'd be a nice little fish soup
provided. The most suitable occupation for
old men.'

'Vladimir Vassilitch!' Evlampia called for
the third time in an incisive tone, and she flung
far away from her the grass she had been
twisting in her fingers, 'I am going!' Her
eyes met mine. 'I am going, Vladimir Vassilievitch!' she repeated, and vanished behind
a bush.

'I'm coming, Evlampia Martinovna, directly!'
shouted Sletkin. 'Martin Petrovitch himself
agrees with us now,' he went on, turning again
to me. 'At first he was offended, certainly,
and even grumbled, until, you know, he realised;
he was, you remember, a hot-tempered violent
man—more's the pity! but there, he's grown
quite meek now. Because he sees his own
interest. Your mamma—mercy on us! how
she pitched into me! . . . To be sure: she's
a lady that sets as much store by her own
authority as Martin Petrovitch used to do.
But you come in and see for yourself. And
you might put in a word when there's an
opportunity. I feel Natalia Nikolaevna's

bounty to me deeply. But we've got to live too.'

'And how was it Zhitkov was refused?' I asked.

'Fedulitch? That dolt?' Sletkin shrugged his shoulders. 'Why, upon my word, what use could he have been? His whole life spent among soldiers—and now he has a fancy to take up farming. He can keep the peasants up to the mark, says he, because he's been used to knocking men about. He can do nothing ; even knocking men about wants some sense. Evlampia Martinovna refused him herself. He was a quite unsuitable person. All our farming would have gone to ruin with him!'

'Coo—y!' sounded Evlampia's musical voice.

'Coming! coming!' Sletkin called back. He held out his hand to me. Though unwillingly, I took it.

'I beg to take leave, Dmitri Semyonovitch,' said Sletkin, showing all his white teeth. 'Shoot wild snipe as much as you like. It's wild game, belonging to no one. But if you come across a hare—you spare it ; that game is ours. Oh, and something else! won't you be having pups from your bitch? I should be obliged for one!'

'Coo—y!' Evlampia's voice rang out again.

'Coo—y!' Sletkin responded, and rushed into the bushes.

XIX

I REMEMBER, when I was left alone, I was absorbed in wondering how it was Harlov had not pounded Sletkin 'into a jelly,' as he said, and how it was Sletkin had not been afraid of such a fate. It was clear Martin Petrovitch really had grown 'meek,' I thought, and I had a still stronger desire to make my way into Eskovo, and get at least a glance at that colossus, whom I could never picture to myself subdued and tractable. I had reached the edge of the copse, when suddenly a big snipe, with a great rush of wings, darted up at my very feet, and flew off into the depths of the wood. I took aim; my gun missed fire. I was greatly annoyed; it had been such a fine bird, and I made up my mind to try if I couldn't make it rise a second time. I set off in the direction of its flight, and going some two hundred paces off into the wood I caught sight—in a little glade, under an overhanging birch-tree—not of the snipe, but of the same Sletkin once more. He was lying on his back, with both hands under his head, and with a smile of contentment gazing upwards at the sky, swinging his left leg, which was crossed over his right knee. He did not notice my approach. A few paces from him, Evlampia was walking slowly up and down the little glade, with downcast eyes. It seemed as though she were looking for something in the grass—mushrooms or something ; now and then, she stooped and stretched out her hand. She was singing in a low voice. I stopped at once, and fell to listening. At first I could not make out what it was she was singing, but afterwards I recognised clearly the following well-known lines of the old ballad :

> ' Hither, hither, threatening storm-cloud,
>   Slay for me the father-in-law,
>   Strike for me the mother-in-law,
>   The young wife I will kill myself ! '

Evlampia sang louder and louder; the last words she delivered with peculiar energy. Sletkin still lay on his back and laughed to himself, while she seemed all the time to be moving round and round him.

'Oh, indeed!' he commented at last. 'The things that come into some people's heads!'

'What?' queried Evlampia.

Sletkin raised his head a little. 'What? Why, what words were those you were uttering?'

'Why, you know, Volodya, one can't leave

the words out of a song,' answered Evlampia, and she turned and saw me. We both cried out aloud at once, and both rushed away in opposite directions.

I made my way hurriedly out of the copse, and crossing a narrow clearing, found myself facing Harlov's garden.

XX

I HAD no time, nor would it have been of any use, to deliberate over what I had seen. Only an expression kept recurring to my mind, 'love spell,' which I had lately heard, and over the signification of which I had pondered a good deal. I walked alongside the garden fence, and in a few moments, behind the silver poplars (they had not yet lost a single leaf, and the foliage was luxuriantly thick and brilliantly glistening), I saw the yard and two little lodges of Martin Petrovitch's homestead. The whole place struck me as having been tidied up and pulled into shape. On every side one could perceive traces of unflagging and severe supervision. Anna Martinovna came out on to the steps, and screwing up her blue-grey eyes, gazed for a long while in the direction of the copse.

'Have you seen the master?' she asked a peasant, who was walking across the yard.

'Vladimir Vassilitch?' responded the latter, taking his cap off. 'He went into the copse, surely.'

'I know, he went to the copse. Hasn't he come back? Haven't you seen him?'

'I 've not seen him . . . nay.'

The peasant continued standing bareheaded before Anna Martinovna.

'Well, you can go,' she said. 'Or no—— wait a bit—— where's Martin Petrovitch? Do you know?'

'Oh, Martin Petrovitch,' answered the peasant, in a sing-song voice, alternately lifting his right and then his left hand, as though pointing away somewhere, 'is sitting yonder, at the pond, with a fishing-rod. He's sitting in the reeds, with a rod. Catching fish, maybe, God knows.'

'Very well . . . you can go,' repeated Anna Martinovna; 'and put away that wheel, it's lying about.'

The peasant ran to carry out her command, while she remained standing a few minutes longer on the steps, still gazing in the direction of the copse. Then she clenched one fist menacingly, and went slowly back into the house. 'Axiutka!' I heard her imperious voice calling within.

Anna Martinovna looked angry, and tightened her lips, thin enough at all times, with a sort of special energy. She was care-lessly dressed, and a coil of loose hair had fallen down on to her shoulder. But in spite of the negligence of her attire, and her irritable humour, she struck me, just as before, as attractive, and I should have been delighted to kiss the narrow hand which looked malignant too, as she twice irritably pushed back the loose tress.

XXI

'CAN Martin Petrovitch have really taken to fishing?' I asked myself, as I turned towards the pond, which was on one side of the garden. I got on to the dam, looked in all directions. . . . Martin Petrovitch was nowhere to be seen. I bent my steps along one of the banks of the pond, and at last, at the very top of it, in a little creek, in the midst of flat broken-down stalks of reddish reed, I caught sight of a huge greyish mass. . . . I looked intently: it was Harlov. Bareheaded, unkempt, in a cotton smock torn at the seams, with his legs crossed under him, he was sitting motionless on the bare earth. So motionless was he that a sandpiper, at my approach, darted up from the dry mud a couple of paces from him, and flew with a flash of its little wings and a whistle over the surface of the water, showing that no one had moved to frighten him for a long while. Harlov's whole appearance was so extraordinary that my dog stopped short directly it saw him, lifted its tail, and growled. He turned his head a very little, and fixed his wild-looking eyes on me and my dog. He was greatly changed by his beard, though it was short, but thick and curly, in white tufts, like Astrachan fur. In his right hand lay the end of a rod, while the other end hovered feebly over the water. I felt an involuntary pang at my heart. I plucked up my spirits, however, went up to him, and wished him good morning. He slowly blinked as though just awake.

'What are you doing, Martin Petrovitch, I began, 'catching fish here?'

'Yes . . . fish,' he answered huskily, and pulled up the rod, on which there fluttered a piece of line, a fathom length, with no hook on it.

'Your tackle is broken off,' I observed, and noticed the same moment that there was no sign of bait-tin nor worms near Martin Petrovitch. . . . And what sort of fishing could there be in September?

'Broken off?' he said, and he passed his hand over his face. 'But it's all the same!'

He dropped the rod in again.

'Natalia Nikolaevna's son?' he asked me, after the lapse of two minutes, during which I had been gazing at him with secret bewilderment. Though he had grown terribly thinner, still he seemed a giant. But what rags he was dressed in, and how utterly he had gone to pieces altogether!

'Yes,' I answered, 'I'm the son of Natalia Nikolaevna B.'

'Is she well?'

'My mother is quite well. She was very much hurt at your refusal,' I added; 'she did not at all expect you would not wish to come and see her.'

Martin Petrovitch's head sank on his breast. 'Have you been there?' he asked, with a motion of his head.

'Where?'

'There, at the house. Haven't you? Go! What is there for you to do here? Go! It's useless talking to me. I don't like it.'

He was silent for a while.

'You'd like to be always idling about with a gun! In my young days I used to be inclined the same way too. Only my father was strict and made me respect him too. Mind you, very different from fathers now-a-days. My father flogged me with a horsewhip, and that was the end of it! I'd to give up idling about! And so I respected him. . . . Oo! . . . Yes! . . .'

Harlov paused again.

'Don't you stop here,' he began again. 'You go along to the house. Things are managed there now—it's first-rate. Volodka'... Here he faltered for a second. 'Our Volodka's a good hand at everything. He's a fine fellow! yes, indeed, and a fine scoundrel too!'

94

I did not know what to say; Martin Petrovitch spoke very tranquilly.

'And you go and see my daughters. You remember, I daresay, I had daughters. They're managers too ... clever ones. But I'm growing old, my lad; I'm on the shelf. Time to repose, you know. ...'

'Nice sort of repose!' I thought, glancing round. 'Martin Petrovitch!' I uttered aloud, 'you really must come and see us.'

Harlov looked at me. 'Go along, my lad, I tell you.'

'Don't hurt mamma's feelings; come and see us.'

'Go away, my lad, go away,' persisted Harlov. 'What do you want to talk to me for?'

'If you have no carriage, mamma will send you hers.'

'Go along!'

'But, really and truly, Martin Petrovitch!'

Harlov looked down again, and I fancied that his cheeks, dingy as though covered with earth, faintly flushed.

'Really, do come,' I went on. 'What's the use of your sitting here? of your making yourself miserable?'

'Making myself miserable?' he commented hesitatingly.

'Yes, to be sure—making yourself miserable!' I repeated.

Harlov said nothing, and seemed lost in

musing. Emboldened by his silence, I determined to be open, to act straightforwardly, bluntly. (Do not forget, I was only fifteen then.)

'Martin Petrovitch!' I began, seating myself beside him. 'I know everything, you see, positively everything. I know how your son-in-law is treating you—doubtless with the consent of your daughters. And now you are in such a position . . . But why lose heart?'

Harlov still remained silent, and simply dropped in his line; while I—what a sensible fellow, what a sage I felt!

'Doubtless,' I began again, 'you acted imprudently in giving up everything to your daughters. It was most generous on your part, and I am not going to blame you. In our days it is a quality only too rare! But since your daughters are so ungrateful, you ought to show a contempt—yes, a contempt—for them . . . and not fret——'

'Stop!' muttered Harlov suddenly, gnashing his teeth, and his eyes, staring at the pond, glittered wrathfully . . . 'Go away!'

'But, Martin Petrovitch——'

'Go away, I tell you, . . . or I'll kill you!'

I had come quite close to him; but at the last words I instinctively jumped up. 'What did you say, Martin Petrovitch?'

'I'll kill you, I tell you; go away!' With a wild moan, a roar, the words broke from

Harlov's breast, but he did not turn his head, and still stared wrathfully straight in front of him. 'I'll take you and fling you and your fool's counsel into the water. You shall learn to pester the old, little milksop!'

'He's gone mad!' flashed through my mind.

I looked at him more attentively, and was completely petrified; Martin Petrovitch was weeping!! Tear after tear rolled from his eyelashes down his cheeks . . . while his face had assumed an expression utterly savage. . . .

'Go away!' he roared once more, 'or I'll kill you, by God! for an example to others!'

He was shaking all over from side to side, and showing his teeth like a wild boar. I snatched up my gun and took to my heels. My dog flew after me, barking. He, too, was frightened.

When I got home, I naturally did not, by so much as a word, to my mother, hint at what I had seen; but coming across Souvenir, I told him—the devil knows why—all about it. That loathsome person was so delighted at my story, shrieking with laughter, and even dancing with pleasure, that I could hardly forbear striking him.

'Ah! I should like,' he kept repeating breathless with laughter, 'to see that fiend, the Swede, Harlov, crawling into the mud and sitting in it. . . .'

'Go over to the pond if you're so curious.'

'Yes ; but how if he kills me?'

I felt horribly sick at Souvenir, and regretted my ill-timed confidence. . . . Zhitkov, to whom he repeated my tale, looked at the matter somewhat differently.

'We shall have to call in the police,' he concluded, 'or, may be, we may have to send for a battalion of military.'

His forebodings with regard to the military battalion did not come true ; but something extraordinary really did happen.

XXII

IN the middle of October, three weeks after
my interview with Martin Petrovitch, I was
standing at the window of my own room in
the second storey of our house, and thinking
of nothing at all, I looked disconsolately into
the yard and the road that lay beyond it.
The weather had been disgusting for the last
five days. Shooting was not even to be thought
of. All things living had hidden themselves;
even the sparrows made no sound, and the
rooks had long ago disappeared from sight. The
wind howled drearily, then whistled spasmodically. The low-hanging sky, unbroken by one
streak of light, had changed from an unpleasant
whitish to a leaden and still more sinister hue;
and the rain, which had been pouring and
pouring, mercilessly and unceasingly, had suddenly become still more violent and more
driving, and streamed with a rushing sound
over the panes. The trees had been stripped
utterly bare, and turned a sort of grey. It
seemed they had nothing left to plunder;
yet the wind would not be denied, but set to

harassing them once more. Puddles, clogged with dead leaves, stood everywhere. Big bubbles, continually bursting and rising up again, leaped and glided over them. Along the roads, the mud lay thick and impassable. The cold pierced its way indoors through one's clothes to the very bones. An involuntary shiver passed over the body, and how sick one felt at heart! Sick, precisely, not sad. It seemed there would never again in the world be sunshine, nor brightness, nor colour, but this rain and mire and grey damp, and raw fog would last for ever, and for ever would the wind whine and moan! Well, I was standing moodily at my window, and I remember a sudden darkness came on—a bluish darkness—though the clock only pointed to twelve. Suddenly I fancied I saw a bear dash across our yard from the gates to the steps! Not on all-fours, certainly, but as he is depicted when he gets up on his hind-paws. I could not believe my eyes. If it were not a bear I had seen, it was, any way, something enormous, black, shaggy. . . . I was still lost in wonder as to what it could be, when suddenly I heard below a furious knocking. It seemed something utterly unlooked for, something terrible was stumbling headlong into our house. Then began a commotion, a hurrying to and fro. . . .

I quickly went down the stairs, ran into the dining-room. . . .

At the drawing-room door facing me stood my mother, as though rooted to the spot. Behind her, peered several scared female faces. The butler, two footmen, and a page, with his mouth wide open with astonishment, were packed together in the doorway of the hall. In the middle of the dining-room, covered with mire, dishevelled, tattered, and soaking wet—so wet that steam rose all round and water was running in little streams over the floor—knelt, shaking ponderously, as it were, at the last gasp . . . the very monster I had seen dashing across the yard! And who was this monster? Harlov! I came up on one side, and saw, not his face, but his head, which he was clutching, with both hands in the hair that blinded him with filth. He was breathing heavily, brokenly; something positively rattled in his throat—and in all the bespattered dark mass, the only thing that could be clearly distinguished was the tiny whites of the eyes, straying wildly about. He was awful! The dignitary came into my mind whom he had once crushed for comparing him to a mastodon. Truly, so might have looked some antediluvian creature that had just escaped another more powerful monster, attacking it in the eternal slime of the primeval swamps.

'Martin Petrovitch!' my mother cried at last, and she clasped her hands. 'Is that you? Good God! Merciful heavens!'

'I . . . I . . .' we heard a broken voice, which seemed with effort and painfully to dwell on each sound. 'Alas! It is I!'

'But what has happened to you? Mercy upon us!'

'Natalia Nikolaev . . . na . . . I have . . . run straight . . . to you . . . from home . . . on foot.' . . .

'Through such mud! But you don't look like a man. Get up; sit down, anyway. . . . And you,' she turned to the maid-servants, 'run quick for cloths. And haven't you some dry clothes?' she asked the butler.

The butler gesticulated as though to say, Is it likely for such a size? . . . 'But we could get a coverlet,' he replied, 'or, there's a new horse-rug.'

'But get up, get up, Martin Petrovitch, sit down,' repeated my mother.

'They've turned me out, madam,' Harlov moaned suddenly, and he flung his head back and stretched his hands out before him. 'They've turned me out, Natalia Nikolaevna! My own daughters, out of my own home.' . . .

My mother sighed and groaned.

'What are you saying? Turned you out! What wickedness! what wickedness!' (She crossed herself.) 'But do get up, Martin Petrovitch, I beg you!'

Two maid-servants came in with cloths and stood still before Harlov. It was clear they did not know how to attack this mountain of filth. 'They have turned me out, madam, they have turned me out!' Harlov kept repeating meanwhile. The butler returned with a large woollen coverlet, and he, too, stood still in perplexity. Souvenir's little head was thrust in at a door and vanished again.

'Martin Petrovitch! get up! Sit down! and tell me everything properly,' my mother commanded in a tone of determination.

Harlov rose. . . . The butler tried to assist him but only dirtied his hand, and, shaking his fingers, retreated to the door. Staggering and faltering, Harlov got to a chair and sat down. The maids again approached him with their cloths, but he waved them off with his hand, and refused the coverlet. My mother did not herself, indeed, insist; to dry Harlov was obviously out of the question; they contented themselves with hastily wiping up his traces on the floor.

XXIII

'HOW have they turned you out?' my mother asked, as soon as he had a little time to recover himself.

'Madam! Natalia Nikolaevna!' he began, in a strained voice,—and again I was struck by the uneasy straying of his eyes; 'I will tell you the truth; I am myself most of all to blame.'

'Ay, to be sure; you would not listen to me at the time,' assented my mother, sinking into an arm-chair and slightly moving a scented handkerchief before her nose; very strong was the smell that came from Harlov . . . the odour in a forest bog is not so strong.

'Alas! that's not where I erred, madam, but through pride. Pride has been my ruin, as it ruined the Tsar Navuhodonosor. I fancied God had given me my full share of sense, and if I resolved on anything, it followed it was right; so . . . and then the fear of death came . . . I was utterly confounded! "I'll show," said I, "to the last, my power and my strength! I'll bestow all on them,—and they must feel it all their lives. . . ."' (Harlov suddenly was shaking all over. . . .) 'Like a mangy dog they have driven me out of the house! This is their gratitude!'

'In what way——,' my mother was beginning. . . .

'They took my page, Maximka, from me,' Harlov interrupted her (his eyes were still wandering, he held both hands—the fingers interlaced—under his chin), 'my carriage they took away, my monthly allowance they cut down, did not pay me the sum specified, cut me short all round, in fact; still I said nothing, bore it all! And I bore it by reason . . . alas! of my pride again. That my cruel enemies might not say, "See, the old fool's sorry for it now"; and you too, do you remember, madam had warned me; "mind you, it's all to no purpose," you said! and so I bore it. . . . Only, to-day I came into my room, and it was occupied already, and my bed they'd thrown out into the lumber-room! "You can sleep there; we put up with you there even only out of charity; we've need of your room for the household." And this was said to me by whom? Volodka Sletkin! the vile hound, the base cur!'

Harlov's voice broke.

'But your daughters? What did they do?' asked my mother.

'But I bore it all,' Harlov went on again; 'bitterness, bitterness was in my heart, let me

tell you, and shame. . . . I could not bear to
look upon the light of day! That was why I
was unwilling to come and see you, ma'am,
from this same feeling, from shame for my
disgrace! I have tried everything, my good
friend; kindness, affection, and threats, and I
reasoned with them, and more besides! I
bowed down before them . . . like this.' (Harlov showed how he had bowed down.) 'And
all in vain. And all of it I bore! At the
beginning, at first, I'd very different thoughts;
I'll up, I thought, and kill them. I'll crush
them all, so that not a trace remains of them!
. . . I'll let them know! Well, but after, I
submitted! It's a cross, I thought, laid upon
me; it's to bid me make ready for death.
And all at once, to-day, driven out, like a cur!
And by whom? Volodka! And you asked
about my daughters; they've no will of their
own at all. They're Volodka's slaves! Yes!'

My mother wondered. 'In Anna's case I
can understand that; she's a wife. . . . But
how comes it your second . . .'

'Evlampia? She's worse than Anna! She's
altogether given herself up into Volodka's
hands. That's the reason she refused your
soldier, too. At his, at Volodka's bidding.
Anna, to be sure, ought to resent it, and she
can't bear her sister, but she submits! He's
bewitched them, the cursed scoundrel! Though
she, Anna, I daresay, is pleased to think that

Evlampia, who was always so proud,—and now see what she's come to! . . . O . . . alas . . . alas! God, my God!'

My mother looked uneasily towards me. I moved a little away as a precautionary measure, for fear I should be sent away altogether. . . .

'I am very sorry indeed, Martin Petrovitch,' she began, 'that my former protégé has caused you so much sorrow, and has turned out so badly. But I, too, was mistaken in him. . . . Who could have expected this of him?'

'Madam,' Harlov moaned out, and he struck himself a blow on the chest, 'I cannot bear the ingratitude of my daughters! I cannot, madam! You know I gave them everything, everything! And besides, my conscience has been tormenting me. Many things . . . alas! many things I have thought over, sitting by the pond, fishing. "If you'd only done good to any one in your life!" was what I pondered upon, "succoured the poor, set the peasants free, or something, to atone for having wrung their lives out of them. You must answer for them before God! Now their tears are re-venged." And what sort of life have they now? It was a deep pit even in my time—why disguise my sins?—but now there's no seeing the bottom! All these sins I have taken upon my soul; I have sacrificed my conscience for my children, and for this I'm laughed to scorn! Kicked out of the house, like a cur!'

'Don't think about that, Martin Petrovitch,' observed my mother.

'And when he told me, your Volodka,' Harlov went on with fresh force, 'when he told me I was not to live in my room any more,— I laid every plank in that room with my own hands,—when he said that to me,—God only knows what passed within me! It was all confusion in my head, and like a knife in my heart. . . . Either to cut his throat or get away out of the house! . . . So, I have run to you, my benefactress, Natalia Nikolaevna . . . where had I to lay my head? And then the rain, the filth . . . I fell down twenty times, maybe! And now . . . in such unseemly . . .'

Harlov scanned himself and moved restlessly in his chair, as though intending to get up.

'Say no more, Martin Petrovitch,' my mother interposed hurriedly; 'what does that signify? That you've made the floor dirty? That's no great matter! Come, I want to make you a proposition. Listen! They shall take you now to a special room, and make you up a clean bed,—you undress, wash, and lie down and sleep a little. . . .'

'Natalia Nikolaevna! There's no sleeping for me!' Harlov responded drearily. 'It's as though there were hammers beating in my brain! Me! like some good-for-nothing beast! . . .'

'Lie down and sleep,' my mother repeated

insistently. 'And then we'll give you some tea,—yes, and we'll have a talk. Don't lose heart, old friend! If they've driven you out of *your* house, in *my* house you will always find a home. . . . I have not forgotten, you know, that you saved my life.'

'Benefactress!' moaned Harlov, and he covered his face with his hand. '*You* must save me now!'

This appeal touched my mother almost to tears. 'I am ready and eager to help you, Martin Petrovitch, in everything I am able. But you must promise me that you will listen to me in future and dismiss every evil thought from you.'

Harlov took his hands from his face. 'If need be,' he said, 'I can forgive them, even!'

My mother nodded her head approvingly. 'I am very glad to see you in such a truly Christian frame of mind, Martin Petrovitch; but we will talk of that later. Meanwhile, you put yourself to rights, and, most of all, sleep. Take Martin Petrovitch to what was the master's room, the green room,' said my mother, addressing the butler, 'and whatever he asks for, let him have it on the spot! Give orders for his clothes to be dried and washed, and ask the housekeeper for what linen is needed. Do you hear?'

'Yes, madam,' responded the butler.

'And as soon as he's asleep tell the tailor

to take his measure; and his beard will have to be shaved.   Not at once, but after.'

'Yes, madam,' repeated the butler.   'Martin Petrovitch, kindly come.'   Harlov got up, looked at my mother, was about to go up to her, but stopped, swinging a bow from the waist, crossed himself three times to the image, and followed the steward.   Behind him, I, too, slipped out of the room.

XXIV

THE butler conducted Harlov to the green room, and at once ran off for the wardroom maid, as it turned out there were no sheets on the bed. Souvenir, who met us in the passage, and popped into the green room with us, promptly proceeded to dance, grinning and chuckling, round Harlov, who stood, his arms held a little away from him, and his legs apart, in the middle of the room, seeming lost in thought. The water was still dripping from him.

'The Swede! The Swede, Harlus!' piped Souvenir, doubling up and holding his sides. 'Mighty founder of the illustrious race of Harlovs, look down on thy descendant! What does he look like? Dost thou recognise him? Ha, ha, ha! Your excellency, your hand, I beg; why, have you got on black gloves?'

I tried to restrain Souvenir, to put him to shame . . . but it was too late for that now.

'He called me parasite, toady! "You've no roof," said he, "to call your own." But now, no doubt about it, he's become as dependent as

poor little me. Martin Petrovitch and Souvenir,
the poor toady, are equal now. He'll have to
live on charity too. They'll toss him the stale
and dirty crust, that the dog has sniffed at and
refused. . . . And they'll tell him to eat it, too.
Ha, ha, ha!'

Harlov still stood motionless, his head drawn
in, his legs and arms held a little apart.

'Martin Harlov, a nobleman born!' Souvenir
went on shrieking. 'What airs he used to give
himself. Just look at me! Don't come near, or
I'll knock you down! . . . And when he was
so clever as to give away and divide his property, didn't he crow! "Gratitude! . . ." he
cackled, "gratitude!" But why were you so
mean to me? Why didn't you make me a
present? May be, I should have felt it more.
And you see I was right when I said they'd
strip you bare, and . . .'

'Souvenir!' I screamed; but Souvenir was
in nowise daunted. Harlov still did not stir.
It seemed as though he were only now beginning to be aware how soaking wet everything
was that he had on, and was waiting to be
helped off with his clothes. But the butler had
not come back.

'And a military man too!' Souvenir began
again. 'In the year twelve, he saved his country;
he showed proofs of his valour. I see how it
is. Stripping the frozen marauders of their
breeches is work he's quite equal to, but when

the hussies stamp their feet at him he's frightened out of his skin.'

'Souvenir! I screamed a second time.

Harlov looked askance at Souvenir. Till that instant he seemed not to have noticed his presence, and only my exclamation aroused his attention.

'Look out, brother,' he growled huskily, 'don't dance yourself into trouble.'

Souvenir fairly rolled about with laughter. 'Ah, how you frighten me, most honoured brother. You're a formidable person, to be sure. You must comb your hair, at any rate, or, God forbid, it'll get dry, and you'll never wash it clean again ; you'll have to mow it with a sickle.' Souvenir all of a sudden got into a fury. 'And you give yourself airs still. A poor outcast, and he gives himself airs. Where's your home now? you'd better tell me that, you were always boasting of it. "I have a home of my own," he used to say, but you're homeless. "My ancestral roof," he would say.' Souvenir pounced on this phrase as an inspiration.

'Mr. Bitchkov,' I protested. 'What are you about? you forget yourself.'

But he still persisted in chattering, and still danced and pranced up and down quite close to Harlov. And still the butler and the ward-room maid did not come.

I felt alarmed. I began to notice that Harlov, who had, during his conversation with my mother, gradually grown quieter, and even towards the end apparently resigned himself to his fate, was beginning to get worked up again. He breathed more hurriedly, it seemed as though his face were suddenly swollen under his ears, his fingers twitched, his eyes again began moving restlessly in the dark mask of his grim face. . . .

'Souvenir, Souvenir!' I cried. 'Stop it, I'll tell mamma.'

But Souvenir seemed possessed by frenzy. 'Yes, yes, most honoured brother,' he began again, 'here we find ourselves, you and I, in the most delicate position. While your daughters, with your son-in-law, Vladimir Vassilievitch, are having a fine laugh at you under your roof. And you should at least curse them, as you promised. Even that you're not equal to. To be sure, how could you hold your own with Vladimir Vassilievitch? Why, you used to call him Volodka, too. You call him Volodka. *He* is Vladimir Vassilievitch, Mr. Sletkin, a landowner, a gentleman, while—what are you, pray?'

A furious roar drowned Souvenir's words. . . . Harlov was aroused. His fists were clenched and lifted, his face was purple, there was foam on his drawn lips, he was shaking with rage. 'Roof, you say!' he thundered in his iron voice, 'curse, you say. . . . No! I will not curse them. . . . They don't care for that . . . But the roof

. . . I will tear the roof off them, and they shall have no roof over their heads, like me. They shall learn to know Martin Harlov. My strength is not all gone yet; they shall learn to laugh at me! . . . They shall have no roof over their heads!'

I was stupefied; never in my life had I witnessed such boundless anger. Not a man—a wild beast—paced to and fro before me. I was stupefied . . . as for Souvenir, he had hidden under the table in his fright.

'They shall not!' Harlov shouted for the last time, and almost knocking over the butler and the wardroom maid, he rushed away out of the house. . . . He dashed headlong across the yard, and vanished through the gates.

XXV

My mother was terribly angry when the butler came with an abashed countenance to report Martin Petrovitch's sudden and unexpected retreat. He did not dare to conceal the cause of this retreat: I was obliged to confirm his story. 'Then it was all your doing!' my mother cried, at the sight of Souvenir, who had run in like a hare, and was even approaching to kiss her hand: 'Your vile tongue is to blame for it all!' 'Excuse me, d'rectly, d'rectly . . .' faltered Souvenir, stuttering and drawing back his elbows behind him. 'D'rectly, . . . d'rectly . . . I know your "d'rectly,"' my mother repeated reprovingly, and she sent him out of the room. Then she rang the bell, sent for Kvitsinsky, and gave him orders to set off on the spot to Eskovo, with a carriage, to find Martin Petrovitch at all costs, and to bring him back. 'Do not let me see you without him,' she concluded. The gloomy Pole bowed his head without a word, and went away.

I went back to my own room, sat down again at the window, and I pondered a long while, I remember, on what had taken place before my eyes. I was puzzled ; I could not understand how it was that Harlov, who had endured the insults of his own family almost without a murmur, had lost all self-control, and been unable to put up with the jeers and pin-pricks of such an abject creature as Souvenir. I did not understand in those days what insufferable bitterness there may sometimes be in a foolish taunt, even when it comes from lips one scorns. . . . The hated name of Sletkin, uttered by Souvenir, had been like a spark thrown into powder. The sore spot could not endure this final prick.

About an hour passed by. Our coach drove into the yard ; but our steward sat in it alone. And my mother had said to him—'don't let me see you without him.' Kvitsinsky jumped hurriedly out of the carriage, and ran up the steps. His face had a perturbed look—something very unusual with him. I promptly rushed downstairs, and followed at his heels into the drawing-room. 'Well? have you brought him ?' asked my mother.

'I have not brought him,' answered Kvitsinsky—'and I could not bring him.'

'How 's that? Have you seen him ?'

'Yes.'

'What has happened to him ? A fit ?'

'No ; nothing has happened.'

'How is it you didn't bring him ?'

'He's pulling his house to pieces.'

'What?'

'He's standing on the roof of the new building, and pulling it to pieces. Forty boards or more, I should guess, must have come down by now, and some five of the rafters too.' ('They shall not have a roof over their heads.' Harlov's words came back to me.)

My mother stared at Kvitsinsky. 'Alone . . . he's standing on the roof, and pulling the roof down?'

'Exactly so. He is walking about on the flooring of the garret in the roof, and smashing right and left of him. His strength, you are aware, madam, is superhuman. And the roof too, one must say, is a poor affair; half-inch deal battens, laid wide apart, one inch nails.'

My mother looked at me, as though wishing to make sure whether she had heard aright. 'Half-inches wide apart,' she repeated, obviously not understanding the meaning of one word. 'Well, what then?' she said at last.

'I have come for instructions. There's no doing anything without men to help. The peasants there are all limp with fright.'

'And his daughters—what of them?'

'His daughters are doing nothing. They're running to and fro, shouting . . . this and that . . . all to no purpose.'

'And is Sletkin there?'

'He's there too. He's making more outcry than all of them—but he can't do anything.'

'And Martin Petrovitch is standing on the roof?'

'On the roof . . . that is, in the garret—and pulling the roof to pieces.'

'Yes, yes,' said my mother, 'half-inches wide apart.'

The position was obviously a serious one. What steps were to be taken? Send to the town for the police captain? Get together the peasants? My mother was quite at her wits' end. Zhitkov, who had come in to dinner, was nonplussed too. It is true, he made another reference to a battalion of military; he offered no advice, however, but confined himself to looking submissive and devoted. Kvitsinsky, seeing he would not get at any instructions, suggested to my mother—with the contemptuous respectfulness peculiar to him—that if she would authorise him to take a few of the stable-boys, gardeners, and other house-serfs, he would make an effort . . .

'Yes, yes,' my mother cut him short, 'do make an effort, dear Vikenty Osipitch! Only make haste, please, and I will take all responsibility on myself!'

Kvitsinsky smiled coldly. 'One thing let me make clear, madam, beforehand; it's impossible to reckon on any result, seeing that Mr. Harlov's strength is so great, and he is so desperate too ; he feels himself to have been very cruelly wronged ! '

' Yes, yes,' my mother assented ; 'and it's all that vile Souvenir's fault ! Never will I forgive him for it. Go and take the servants and set off, Vikenty Osipitch ! '

' You'd better take plenty of cord, Mr. Steward, and some fire-escape tackle,' Zhitkov brought out in his bass—'and if there is such a thing as a net, it would be as well to take that along too. We once had in our regiment . . .'

' Kindly refrain from instructing me, sir,' Kvitsinsky cut him short, with an air of vexation ; ' I know what is needed without your aid.'

Zhitkov was offended, and protested that as he imagined he, too, was called upon . . .

' No, no ! ' interposed my mother ; ' you'd better stop where you are . . . Let Vikenty Osipitch act alone . . . Make haste, Vikenty Osipitch ! '

Zhitkov was still more offended, while Kvitsinsky bowed and went out.

I rushed off to the stable, hurriedly saddled my horse myself, and set off at a gallop along the road to Eskovo.

XXVI

THE rain had ceased, but the wind was blowing with redoubled force—straight into my face. Half-way there, the saddle almost slipped round under me; the girth had got loose; I got off and tried to tighten the straps with my teeth. . . . All at once I heard some-one calling me by my name . . . Souvenir was running towards me across the green fields. 'What!' he shouted to me from some way off, 'was your curiosity too much for you? But it's no use . . . I went over there, straight, at Harlov's heels . . . Such a state of things you never saw in your life!'

'You want to enjoy what you have done,' I said indignantly, and, jumping on my horse, I set off again at a gallop. But the indefatigable Souvenir did not give me up, and chuckled and grinned, even as he ran. At last, Eskovo was reached—there was the dam, and there the long hedge and willow-tree of the homestead . . . I rode up to the gate, dismounted, tied up my horse, and stood still in amazement.

Of one third of the roof of the newer house, of the front part, nothing was left but the skeleton ; boards and litter lay in disorderly heaps on the ground on both sides of the building. Even supposing the roof to be, as Kvitsinsky had said, a poor affair, even so, it was something incredible! On the floor of the garret, in a whirl of dust and rubbish, a blackish grey mass was moving to and fro with rapid ungainly action, at one moment shaking the remaining chimney, built of brick, (the other had fallen already) then tearing up the boarding and flinging it down below, then clutching at the very rafters. It was Harlov. He struck me as being exactly like a bear at this moment too; the head, and back, and shoulders were a bear's, and he put his feet down wide apart without bending the insteps —also like a bear. The bitter wind was blowing upon him from every side, lifting his matted locks. It was horrible to see, here and there, red patches of bare flesh through the rents in his tattered clothes ; it was horrible to hear his wild husky muttering. There were a lot of people in the yard ; peasant-women, boys, and servant-girls stood close along the hedge. A few peasants huddled together in a separate group, a little way off. The old village priest, whom I knew, was standing, bareheaded, on the steps of the other house, and holding a brazen cross in both hands, from time to time, silently and hopelessly, raised it, and, as it were, showed it to Harlov. Beside the priest, stood Evlampia with her back against the wall, gazing fixedly at her father. Anna, at one moment, pushed her head out of the little window, then vanished, then hurried into the yard, then went back into the house. Sletkin—pale all over, livid—in an old dressing-gown and smoking-cap, with a single-barrelled rifle in his hands, kept running to and fro with little steps. He had completely *gone Jewish*, as it is called. He was gasping, threatening, shaking, pointing the gun at Harlov, then letting it drop back on his shoulder— pointing it again, shrieking, weeping. . . . On seeing Souvenir and me he simply flew to us.

'Look, look, what is going on here!' he wailed—'look! He's gone out of his mind, he's raving mad . . . and see what he's doing! I've sent for the police already—but no one comes! No one comes! If I do fire at him, the law couldn't touch me, for every man has a right to defend his own property! And I will fire! . . . By God, I'll fire!'

He ran off toward the house.

'Martin Petrovitch, look out! If you don't get down, I'll fire!'

'Fire away!' came a husky voice from the roof. 'Fire away! And meanwhile here's a little present for you!'

A long plank flew up, and, turning over twice in the air, came violently to the earth, just at Sletkin's feet. He positively jumped into the air, while Harlov chuckled.

'Merciful Jesus!' faltered some one behind me. I looked round: Souvenir. 'Ah!' I thought, 'he's left off laughing now!'

Sletkin clutched a peasant, who was standing near, by the collar.

'Climb up now, climb up, climb up, all of you, you devils,' he wailed, shaking the man with all his force, 'save my property!'

The peasant took a couple of steps forward, threw his head back, waved his arms, shouted—'hi! here! master!' shifted from one foot to the other uneasily, and then turned back.

'A ladder! bring a ladder!' Sletkin addressed the other peasants.

'Where are we to get it?' was heard in answer.

'And if we had a ladder,' one voice pronounced deliberately, 'who'd care to climb up? Not such fools! He'd wring your neck for you—in a twinkling!'

'He'd kill one in no time,' said one young lad with flaxen hair and a half-idiotic face.

'To be sure he would,' the others confirmed. It struck me that, even if there had been no obvious danger, the peasants would yet have been loath to carry out their new owner's orders. They almost approved of Harlov, though they were amazed at him.

'Ugh, you robbers!' moaned Sletkin; 'you shall all catch it . . .'

But at this moment, with a heavy rumble, the last chimney came crashing down, and, in the midst of the cloud of yellow dust that flew up instantly, Harlov—uttering a piercing shriek and lifting his bleeding hands high in the air— turned facing us. Sletkin pointed the gun at him again.

Evlampia pulled him back by the elbow.

'Don't interfere!' he snarled savagely at her.

'And you—don't you dare!' she answered; and her blue eyes flashed menacingly under her scowling brows. 'Father's pulling his house down. It's his own.'

'You lie: it's ours!'

'You say ours; but I say it's his.'

Sletkin hissed with fury; Evlampia's eyes seemed stabbing him in the face.

'Ah, how d'ye do! my delightful daughter!' Harlov thundered from above. 'How d'ye do! Evlampia Martinovna! How are you getting on with your sweetheart? Are your kisses sweet, and your fondling?'

'Father!' rang out Evlampia's musical voice.

'Eh, daughter?' answered Harlov; and he came down to the very edge of the wall. His face, as far as I could make it out, wore a strange smile, a bright, mirthful—and for that

125

very reason peculiarly strange and evil—smile.
. . . Many years later I saw just the same
smile on the face of a man condemned to
death.

'Stop, father; come down. We are in fault;
we give everything back to you. Come down.'

'What do you mean by disposing of what's
ours?' put in Sletkin. Evlampia merely scowled
more angrily.

'I give you back my share. I give up
everything. Give over, come down, father!
Forgive us; forgive me.'

Harlov still went on smiling. 'It's too late,
my darling,' he said, and each of his words rang
out like brass. 'Too late your stony heart is
touched! The rock's started rolling downhill—
there's no holding it back now! And don't look
to me now; I'm a doomed man! You'd do
better to look to your Volodka; see what a
pretty fellow you've picked out! And look
to your hellish sister; there's her foxy nose
yonder thrust out of the window; she's peering
yonder after that husband of hers! No, my
good friends; you would rob me of a roof
over my head, so I will leave you not one beam
upon another! With my own hands I built it,
with my own hands I destroy it,—yes, with my
hands alone! See, I've taken no axe to help
me!'

He snorted at his two open hands, and
clutched at the centre beam again.

'Enough, father,' Evlampia was saying meanwhile, and her voice had grown marvellously caressing, 'let bygones be bygones. Come, trust me; you always trusted me. Come, get down; come to me to my little room, to my soft bed. I will dry you and warm you; I will bind up your wounds; see, you have torn your hands. You shall live with me as in Christ's bosom; food shall be sweet to you—and sleep sweeter yet. Come, we have done wrong! yes, we were puffed up, we have sinned; come, forgive!'

Harlov shook his head. 'Talk away! Me believe you! Never again! You've murdered all trust in my heart! You've murdered everything! I was an eagle, and became a worm for you . . . and you,—would you even crush the worm? Have done! I loved you, you know very well,—but now you are no daughter to me, and I'm no father to you . . . I'm a doomed man! Don't meddle! As for you, fire away, coward, mighty man of valour!' Harlov bellowed suddenly at Sletkin. 'Why is it you keep aiming and don't shoot? Are you mindful of the law; if the recipient of a gift commits an attempt upon the life of the giver,' Harlov enunciated distinctly, 'then the giver is empowered to claim everything back again? Ha, ha! don't be afraid, law-abiding man! I'd make no claims. I'll make an end of everything myself. . . Here goes!'

'Father!' for the last time Evlampia besought him.

'Silence!'

'Martin Petrovitch! brother, be generous and forgive!' faltered Souvenir.

'Father! dear father!'

'Silence, bitch!' shouted Harlov. At Souvenir he did not even glance,—he merely spat in his direction.

XXVII

At that instant, Kvitsinsky, with all his retinue
—in three carts—appeared at the gates. The
tired horses panted, the men jumped out, one
after another, into the mud.

'Aha!' Harlov shouted at the top of his
voice. 'An army . . . here it comes, an army!
A whole army they're sending against me!
Capital! Only I give warning—if any one
comes up here to me on the roof, I'll send him
flying down, head over heels! I'm an in-
hospitable master; I don't like visitors at
wrong times! No indeed!'

He was hanging with both hands on to the
front rafters of the roof, the so-called standards
of the gable, and beginning to shake them
violently. Balancing on the edge of the garret
flooring, he dragged them, as it were, after him,
chanting rhythmically like a bargeman, 'One
more pull! one more! o-oh!'

Sletkin ran up to Kvitsinsky and was beginning to whimper and pour out complaints.
. . . The latter begged him 'not to interfere,
and proceeded to carry out the plan he had

evolved. He took up his position in front of the house, and began, by way of diversion, to explain to Harlov that what he was about was unworthy of his rank. . . .

'One more pull! one more!' chanted Harlov.

. . . 'That Natalia Nikolaevna was greatly displeased at his proceedings, and had not expected it of him.' . . .

'One more pull! one more! o-oh!' Harlov chanted . . . while, meantime, Kvitsinsky had despatched the four sturdiest and boldest of the stable-boys to the other side of the house to clamber up the roof from behind. Harlov, however, detected the plan of attack; he suddenly left the standards and ran quickly to the back part of the roof. His appearance was so alarming that the two stable-boys who had already got up to the garret, dropped instantly back again to the ground by the water-pipe, to the great glee of the serf boys, who positively roared with laughter. Harlov shook his fist after them and, going back to the front part of the house, again clutched at the standards and began once more loosening them, singing again, like a bargeman.

Suddenly he stopped, stared. . . .

'Maximushka, my dear! my friend!' he cried; 'is it you?'

I looked round. . . . There, actually, was Maximka, stepping out from the crowd of peasants. Grinning and showing his teeth, he walked forward. His master, the tailor, had probably let him come home for a holiday.

'Climb up to me, Maximushka, my faithful servant,' Harlov went on; 'together let us rid ourselves of evil Tartar folk, of Lithuanian thieves!'

Maximka, still grinning, promptly began climbing up the roof. . . . But they seized him and pulled him back—goodness knows why; possibly as an example to the rest; he could hardly have been much aid to Martin Petrovitch.

'Oh, all right! Good!' Harlov pronounced, in a voice of menace, and again he took hold of the standards.

'Vikenty Osipovitch! with your permission, I'll shoot,' Sletkin turned to Kvitsinsky; 'more to frighten him, see, than anything; my gun's only charged with snipe-shot.' But Kvitsinsky had not time to answer him, when the front couple of standards, viciously shaken in Harlov's iron hands, heeled over with a loud crack and crashed into the yard; and with it, not able to stop himself, came Harlov too, and fell with a heavy thud on the earth. Every one shuddered and drew a deep breath. . . . Harlov lay without stirring on his breast, and on his back lay the top central beam of the roof, which had come down with the falling gable's timbers.

XXVIII

THEY ran up to Harlov, rolled the beam off
him, turned him over on his back. His face
was lifeless, there was blood about his mouth;
he did not seem to breathe. 'The breath is
gone out of him,' muttered the peasants,
standing about him. They ran to the well
for water, brought a whole bucketful, and
drenched Harlov's head. The mud and dust
ran off his face, but he looked as lifeless
as ever. They dragged up a bench, set it
in the house itself, and with difficulty raising
the huge body of Martin Petrovitch, laid
it there with the head to the wall. The
page Maximka approached, fell on one knee,
and, his other leg stretched far behind
him, in a theatrical way, supported his former
master's arm. Evlampia, pale as death,
stood directly facing her father, her great eyes
fastened immovably upon him. Anna and
Sletkin did not come near him. All were
silent, all, as it were, waited for something.

At last we heard broken, smacking noises in Harlov's throat, as though he were swallowing. . . . Then he feebly moved one, his right, hand (Maximka supported the left), opened one, the right eye, and slowly gazing about him, as though drunken with some fearful drunkenness, groaned, articulated, stammering, 'I'm sma-ashed' . . . and as though after a moment's thought, added, 'here it is, the ra . . . aven co . . . olt!' The blood suddenly gushed thickly from his mouth . . . his whole body began to quiver. . . .

'The end!' I thought. . . . But once more Harlov opened the same eye (the left eyelid lay as motionless as on a dead man's face), and fixing it on Evlampia, he articulated, hardly above a breath, 'Well, daugh . . . ter . . . you, I do not . . .'

Kvitsinsky, with a sharp motion of his hand, beckoned to the priest, who was still standing on the step. . . . The old man came up, his narrow cassock clinging about his feeble knees. But suddenly there was a sort of horrible twitching in Harlov's legs and in his stomach too ; an irregular contraction passed upwards over his face. Evlampia's face seemed quivering and working in the same way. Maximka began crossing himself. . . . I was seized with horror; I ran out to the gates, squeezed myself close to them, not looking round. A minute later a soft murmur ran through the crowd, behind my back, and I understood that Martin Petrovitch was no more.

His skull had been fractured by the beam and his ribs injured, as it appeared at the post-mortem examination.

XXIX

WHAT had he wanted to say to her as he lay dying? I asked myself as I went home on my cob: 'I do not . . . forgive,' or 'do not . . . pardon.' The rain had come on again, but I rode at a walking pace. I wanted to be alone as long as possible; I wanted to give myself up to my reflections, unchecked. Souvenir had gone back in one of the carts that had come with Kvitsinsky. Young and frivolous as I was at that time, the sudden sweeping change (not in mere details only) that is invariably called forth in all hearts by the coming of death— expected or unexpected, it makes no difference ! —its majesty, its gravity, and its truthfulness could not fail to impress me. I was impressed too, . . . but for all that, my troubled, childish eyes noted many things at once; they noted how Sletkin, hurriedly and furtively, as though it were something stolen, popped the gun out of sight; how he and his wife became, both of them, instantly the object of a sort of unspoken but universal aloofness. To Evlampia, though her fault was probably no less than her sister's this aloofness did not extend. She even aroused a certain sympathy, when she fell at her dead father's feet. But that she too was guilty, that was none the less felt by all. 'The old man was wronged,' said a grey-haired peasant with a big head, leaning, like some ancient judge, with both hands and his beard on a long staff; 'on your soul lies the sin! You wronged him!' That saying was at once accepted by every one as the final judgment. The peasants' sense of justice found expression in it, I felt that at once. I noticed too that, at the first, Sletkin did not *dare* to give directions. Without him, they lifted up the body and carried it into the other house. Without asking him, the priest went for everything needful to the church, while the village elder ran to the village to send off a cart and horse to the town. Even Anna Martinovna did not venture to use her ordinary imperious tone in ordering the samovar to be brought, 'for hot water, to wash the deceased.' Her orders were more like an entreaty, and she was answered rudely. . . .

I was absorbed all the while by the question, What was it exactly he wanted to say to his daughter? Did he want to forgive her or to curse her? Finally I decided that it was—forgiveness.

Three days later, the funeral of Martin Petrovitch took place. The cost of the ceremony was undertaken by my mother, who was deeply

grieved at his death, and gave orders that no
expense was to be spared. She did not herself
go to the church, because she was unwilling,
as she said, to set eyes on those two vile
hussies and that nasty little Jew. But she
sent Kvitsinsky, me, and Zhitkov, though from
that time forward she always spoke of the latter
as a regular old woman. Souvenir she did not
admit to her presence, and was furious with him
for long after, saying that he was the murderer
of her friend. He felt his disgrace acutely; he
was continually running, on tiptoe, up and down
the room, next to the one where my mother
was; he gave himself up to a sort of scared
and abject melancholy, shuddering and muttering, 'd'rectly!'

In church, and during the procession, Sletkin
struck me as having recovered his self-possession. He gave directions and bustled about in
his old way, and kept a greedy look-out that not
a superfluous farthing should be spent, though
his own pocket was not in question. Maximka,
in a new Cossack dress, also a present from my
mother, gave vent to such tenor notes in the
choir, that certainly no one could have any
doubts as to the sincerity of his devotion to
the deceased. Both the sisters were duly
attired in mourning, but they seemed more
stupefied than grieved, especially Evlampia.
Anna wore a meek, Lenten air, but made no
attempt to weep, and was continually passing

her handsome, thin hand over her hair and cheek. Evlampia seemed deep in thought all the time. The universal, unbending alienation, condemnation, which I had noticed on the day of Harlov's death, I detected now too on the faces of all the people in the church, in their actions and their glances, but still more grave and, as it were, impersonal. It seemed as though all those people felt that the sin into which the Harlov family had fallen—this great sin—had gone now before the presence of the one righteous Judge, and that for that reason, there was no need now for them to trouble themselves and be indignant. They prayed devoutly for the soul of the dead man, whom in life they had not specially liked, whom they had feared indeed. Very abruptly had death overtaken him.

' And it's not as though he had been drinking heavily, brother,' said one peasant to another, in the porch.

' Nay, without drink he was drunken indeed,' responded the other.

' He was cruelly wronged,' the first peasant repeated the phrase that summed it up.

' Cruelly wronged,' the others murmured after him.

' The deceased was a hard master to you, wasn't he?' I asked a peasant, whom I recognised as one of Harlov's serfs.

' He was a master, certainly,' answered

the peasant, 'but still . . . he was cruelly wronged!'

'Cruelly wronged,'. . . I heard again in the crowd.

At the grave, too, Evlampia stood, as it were, lost. Thoughts were torturing her . . . bitter thoughts. I noticed that Sletkin, who several times addressed some remark to her, she treated as she had once treated Zhitkov, and worse still.

Some days later, there was a rumour all over our neighbourhood, that Evlampia Martinovna had left the home of her fathers for ever, leaving all the property that came to her to her sister and brother-in-law, and only taking some hundreds of roubles. . . . 'So Anna's bought her out, it seems!' remarked my mother; 'but you and I, certainly,' she added, addressing Zhitkov, with whom she was playing picquet—he took Souvenir's place, 'are not skilful hands!' Zhitkov looked dejectedly at his mighty palms. . . . 'Hands like that! Not skilful!' he seemed to be saying to himself. . . .

Soon after, my mother and I went to live in Moscow, and many years passed before it was my lot to behold Martin Petrovitch's daughters again.

XXX

But I did see them again. Anna Martinovna
I came across in the most ordinary way.

After my mother's death I paid a visit to our
village, where I had not been for over fifteen
years, and there I received an invitation from
the mediator (at that time the process of settling
the boundaries between the peasants and their
former owners was taking place over the whole
of Russia with a slowness not yet forgotten) to a
meeting of the other landowners of our neighbourhood, to be held on the estate of the widow
Anna Sletkin. The news that my mother's
'nasty little Jew,' with the prune-coloured eyes,
no longer existed in this world, caused me, I confess, no regret whatever. But it was interesting
to get a glimpse of his widow. She had the
reputation in the neighbourhood of a first-rate
manager. And so it proved; her estate and
homestead and the house itself (I could not help
glancing at the roof; it was an iron one) all
turned out to be in excellent order; everything
was neat, clean, tidied-up, where needful—
painted, as though its mistress were a German.

Anna Martinovna herself, of course, looked older. But the peculiar, cold, and, as it were, wicked charm which had once so fascinated me had not altogether left her. She was dressed in rustic fashion, but elegantly. She received us, not cordially—that word was not applicable to her—but courteously, and on seeing me, a witness of that fearful scene, not an eyelash quivered. She made not the slightest reference to my mother, nor her father, nor her sister, nor her husband.

She had two daughters, both very pretty, slim young things, with charming little faces and a bright and friendly expression in their black eyes. There was a son, too, a little like his father, but still a boy to be proud of! During the discussions between the landowners, Anna Martinovna's attitude was composed and dignified, she showed no sign of being specially obstinate, nor specially grasping. But none had a truer perception of their own interests than she of hers; none could more convincingly expound and defend their rights. All the laws 'pertinent to the case,' even the Minister's circulars, she had thoroughly mastered. She spoke little, and in a quiet voice, but every word she uttered was to the point. It ended in our all signifying our agreement to all her demands, and making concessions, which we could only marvel at ourselves. On our way home, some of the

worthy landowners even used harsh words of
themselves; they all hummed and hawed, and
shook their heads.

'Ah, she's got brains that woman!' said one.

'A tricky baggage!' put in another less
delicate proprietor. 'Smooth in word, but
cruel in deed!'

'And a screw into the bargain!' added a
third; 'not a glass of vodka nor a morsel of
caviare for us—what do you think of that?'

'What can one expect of her?' suddenly
croaked a gentleman who had been silent till
then, 'every one knows she poisoned her
husband!'

To my astonishment, nobody thought fit to
controvert this awful and certainly unfounded
charge! I was the more surprised at this, as,
in spite of the slighting expressions I have
reported, all of them felt respect for Anna
Martinovna, not excluding the indelicate landowner. As for the mediator, he waxed positively eloquent.

'Put her on a throne,' he exclaimed, 'she'd
be another Semiramis or Catherine the Second!
The discipline among her peasants is a perfect
model. . . . The education of her children is
model! What a head! What brains!'

Without going into the question of Semiramis
and Catherine, there was no doubt Anna Martinovna was living a very happy life. Ease,
inward and external, the pleasant serenity of

spiritual health, seemed the very atmosphere about herself, her family, all her surroundings. How far she had deserved such happiness . . . that is another question. Such questions, though, are only propounded in youth. Everything in the world, good and bad, comes to man, not through his deserts, but in consequence of some as yet unknown but logical laws which I will not take upon myself to indicate, though I sometimes fancy I have a dim perception of them.

XXXI

I QUESTIONED the mediator about Evlampia
Martinovna, and learnt that she had been lost
sight of completely ever since she left home,
and probably 'had departed this life long ago.'

So our worthy mediator expressed himself
. . . but I am convinced that I *have seen*
Evlampia, that I have come across her. This
was how it was.

Four years after my interview with Anna
Martinovna, I was spending the summer at
Murino, a little hamlet near Petersburg, a
well-known resort of summer visitors of the
middle class. The shooting was pretty decent
about Murino at that time, and I used to go
out with my gun almost every day. I had a
companion on my expeditions, a man of the
tradesman class, called Vikulov, a very sensible
and good-natured fellow ; but, as he said of
himself, of no position whatever. This man
had been simply everywhere, and everything !
Nothing could astonish him, he knew everything—but he cared for nothing but shooting
and wine. Well, one day we were on our way

home to Murino, and we chanced to pass a
solitary house, standing at the cross-roads, and
enclosed by a high, close paling. It was not
the first time I had seen the house, and every
time it excited my curiosity. There was something about it mysterious, locked-up, grimly-
dumb, something suggestive of a prison or a
hospital. Nothing of it could be seen from
the road but its steep, dark, red-painted roof.
There was only one pair of gates in the whole
fence; and these seemed fastened and never
opened. No sound came from the other side
of them. For all that, we felt that some one
was certainly living in the house; it had not
at all the air of a deserted dwelling. On the
contrary, everything about it was stout, and
and tight, and strong, as if it would stand a
siege !

'What is that fortress?' I asked my companion. 'Don't you know?'

Vikulov gave a sly wink. 'A fine building,
eh? The police-captain of these parts gets a
nice little income out of it !'

'How's that ?'

'I'll tell you. You've heard, I daresay, of
the Flagellant dissenters—that do without
priests, you know ?'

'Yes.'

'Well, it's there that their chief mother lives.'

'A woman ?'

'Yes—the mother; a mother of God, they say.'

'Nonsense!'

'I tell you, it is so. She is a strict one, they say. . . . A regular commander-in-chief! She rules over thousands! I'd take her, and all these mothers of God . . . But what's the use of talking?'

He called his Pegashka, a marvellous dog, with an excellent scent, but with no notion of setting. Vikulov was obliged to tie her hind paws to keep her from running so furiously.

His words sank into my memory. I sometimes went out of my way to pass by the mysterious house. One day I had just got up to it, when suddenly—wonderful to relate!—a bolt grated in the gates, a key creaked in the lock, then the gates themselves slowly parted, there appeared a large horse's head, with a plaited forelock under a decorated yoke, and slowly there rolled into the road a small cart, like those driven by horse-dealers, and higglers. On the leather cushion of the cart, near to me, sat a peasant of about thirty, of a remarkably handsome and attractive appearance, in a neat black smock, and a black cap, pulled down low on his forehead. He was carefully driving the well-fed horse, whose sides were as broad as a stove. Beside the peasant, on the far side of the cart, sat a tall woman, as straight as an arrow. Her head was covered by a costly-looking black shawl. She was dressed in a short jerkin of dove-coloured velvet, and a dark blue merino skirt; her white hands she held discreetly clasped on her bosom. The cart turned on the road to the left, and brought the woman within two paces of me; she turned her head a little, and I recognised Evlampia Harlov. I knew her at once, I did not doubt for one instant, and indeed no doubt was possible; eyes like hers, and above all that cut of the lips—haughty and sensual—I had never seen in any one else. Her face had grown longer and thinner, the skin was darker, here and there lines could be discerned; but, above all, the expression of the face was changed! It is difficult to do justice in words to the self-confidence, the sternness, the pride it had gained! Not simply the serenity of power—the satiety of power was visible in every feature. The careless glance she cast at me told of long years of habitually meeting nothing but reverent, unquestioning obedience. That woman clearly lived surrounded, not by worshippers, but by slaves. She had clearly forgotten even the time when any command, any desire of hers, was not carried out at the instant! I called her loudly by her name and her father's; she gave a faint start, looked at me a second time, not with alarm, but with contemptuous wrath, as though asking—'Who dares to disturb me?' and barely parting her lips, uttered a word of command. The peasant sitting beside her started forward, with a wave of his

147

arm struck the horse with the reins—the horse set off at a strong rapid trot, and the cart disappeared.

Since then I have not seen Evlampia again. In what way Martin Petrovitch's daughter came to be a Holy Virgin in the Flagellant sect I cannot imagine. But, who knows, very likely she has founded a sect which will be called—or even now is called—after her name, the Evlampieshtchin sect? Anything may be, anything may come to pass.

And so this is what I had to tell you of my *Lear of the Steppes*, of his family and his doings.

The story-teller ceased, and we talked a little longer, and then parted, each to his home.

WEIMAR, 1870.

FAUST

FAUST

A STORY IN NINE LETTERS

Entbehren sollst du, sollst entbehren (FAUST, PART I.)

FIRST LETTER

FROM PAVEL ALEXANDROVITCH B. . . . TO SEMYON NIKOLAEVITCH V. . . .

M—— VILLAGE, *6th June* 1850.

I HAVE been here for three days, my dear fellow, and, as I promised, I take up my pen to write to you. It has been drizzling with fine rain ever since the morning; I can't go out; and I want a little chat with you, too. Here I am again in my old home, where—it's a dreadful thing to say—I have not been for nine long years. Really, as you may fancy, I have become quite a different man. Yes, utterly different, indeed; do you remember, in the drawing-room, the little tarnished looking-glass of my great-grandmother's, with the queer little curly scrolls in the corners—you always used to be speculating on what it had seen a hundred

151

years ago—directly I arrived, I went up to
it, and I could not help feeling disconcerted. I
suddenly saw how old and changed I had
become in these last years. But I am not
alone in that respect. My little house, which
was old and tottering long ago, will hardly
hold together now, it is all on the slant, and
seems sunk into the ground. My dear Vassilievna, the housekeeper (you can't have forgotten her; she used to regale you with
such capital jam), is quite shrivelled up and
bent; when she saw me, she could not call out,
and did not start crying, but only moaned and
choked, sank helplessly into a chair, and waved
her hand. Old Terenty has some spirit left in
him still; he holds himself up as much as ever,
and turns out his feet as he walks. He still
wears the same yellow nankeen breeches, and
the same creaking goatskin slippers, with high
heels and ribbons, which touched you so much
sometimes, . . . but, mercy on us!—how the
breeches flap about his thin legs nowadays!
how white his hair has grown! and his face
has shrunk up into a sort of little fist. When
he speaks to me, when he begins directing the
servants, and giving orders in the next room, it
makes me laugh and feel sorry for him. All
his teeth are gone, and he mumbles with a
whistling, hissing sound. On the other hand,
the garden has got on wonderfully. The modest
little plants of lilac, acacia, and honeysuckle

(do you remember, we planted them together?) have grown into splendid, thick bushes. The birches, the maples—all that has spread out and grown tall; the avenues of lime-trees are particularly fine. I love those avenues, I love the tender grey, green colour, and the delicate fragrance of the air under their arching boughs; I love the changing network of rings of light on the dark earth—there is no sand here, you know. My favourite oak sapling has grown into a young oak tree. Yesterday I spent more than an hour in the middle of the day on a garden bench in its shade. I felt very happy. All about me the grass was deliciously luxuriant; a rich, soft, golden light lay upon everything; it made its way even into the shade . . . and the birds one could hear! You've not forgotten, I expect, that birds are a passion of mine? The turtle-doves cooed unceasingly; from time to time there came the whistle of the oriole; the chaffinch uttered its sweet little refrain; the blackbirds quarrelled and twittered; the cuckoo called far away; suddenly, like a mad thing, the woodpecker uttered its shrill cry. I listened and listened to this subdued, mingled sound, and did not want to move, while my heart was full of something between languor and tenderness.

And it's not only the garden that has grown up: I am continually coming across sturdy, thick-set lads, whom I cannot recognise as the little boys I used to know in old days. Your favourite, Timosha, has turned into a Timofay, such as you could never imagine. You had fears in those days for his health, and predicted consumption ; but now you should just see his huge, red hands, as they stick out from the narrow sleeves of his nankeen coat, and the stout rounded muscles that stand out all over him! He has a neck like a bull's, and a head all over tight, fair curls—a regular Farnese Hercules. His face, though, has changed less than the others'; it is not even much larger in circumference, and the good-humoured, 'gaping'—as you used to say—smile has remained the same. I have taken him to be my valet ; I got rid of my Petersburg fellow at Moscow ; he was really too fond of putting me to shame, and making me feel the superiority of his Petersburg manners. Of my dogs I have not found one ; they have all passed away. Nefka lived longer than any of them—and she did not live till my return, as Argos lived till the return of Ulysses; she was not fated to look once more with her lustreless eyes on her master and companion in the chase. But Shavka is all right, and barks as hoarsely as ever, and has one ear torn just the same, and burrs sticking to his tail,—all just as it should be. I have taken up my abode in what was your room. It is true the sun beats down upon it, and there are a lot of flies in it ; but there is less of the smell of the old house in it than in

the other rooms. It's a queer thing; that musty,
rather sour, faint smell has a powerful effect on
my imagination; I don't mean that it's disagreeable to me, quite the contrary, but it
produces melancholy, and, at last, depression.
I am very fond, just as you are, of podgy old
chests with brass plates, white armchairs with
oval backs, and crooked legs, fly-blown glass
lustres, with a big egg of lilac tinsel in the
centre—of all sorts of ancestral furniture, in
fact. But I can't stand seeing it all continually;
a sort of agitated dejection (it is just that) takes
possession of me. In the room where I have
established myself, the furniture is of the most
ordinary, home-made description. I have left,
though, in the corner, a long narrow set of
shelves, on which there is an old-fashioned set
of blown green and blue glasses, just discernible
through the dust. And I have had hung on the
wall that portrait of a woman—you remember,
in the black frame?—that you used to call the
portrait of Manon Lescaut. It has got rather
darker in these nine years; but the eyes have the
same pensive, sly, and tender look, the lips have
the same capricious, melancholy smile, and the
half-plucked rose falls as softly as ever from her
slender fingers. I am greatly amused by the
blinds in my room. They were once green,
but have been turned yellow by the sun; on
them are depicted, in dark colours, scenes
from d'Arlencourt's *Hermit*. On one curtain

the hermit, with an immense beard, goggle-eyes, and sandals on his feet, is carrying off a young lady with dishevelled locks to the mountains. On another one, there is a terrific combat going on between four knights wearing birettas, and with puffs on their shoulders; one, much foreshortened, lies slain—in fact, there are pictures of all sorts of horrors, while all about there is such unbroken peace, and the blinds themselves throw such soft light on the ceiling. . . . A sort of inward calm has come upon me since I have been settled here; one wants to do nothing, one wants to see no one, one looks forward to nothing, one is too lazy for thought, but not too lazy for musing; two different things, as you know well. Memories of childhood, at first, came flooding upon me—wherever I went, whatever I looked at, they surged up on all sides, distinct, to the smallest detail, and, as it were, immovable, in their clearly defined outlines. . . . Then these memories were succeeded by others, then . . . then I gradually turned away from the past, and all that was left was a sort of drowsy heaviness in my heart. Fancy! as I was sitting on the dike, under a willow, I suddenly and unexpectedly burst out crying, and should have gone on crying a long while, in spite of my advanced years, if I had not been put to shame by a passing peasant woman, who stared at me with curiosity, then, without turning her face towards me, gave

a low bow from the waist, and passed on. I
should be very glad to remain in the same mood
(I shan't do any more crying, of course) till I
go away from here, that is, till September, and
should be very sorry if any of my neighbours
should take it into his head to call on me.
However there is no danger, I fancy, of that ; I
have no near neighbours here. You will understand me, I 'm sure ; you know yourself, by
experience, how often solitude is beneficial . . .
I need it now after wanderings of all sorts.

But I shan't be dull. I have brought a few
books with me, and I have a pretty fair library
here. Yesterday, I opened all the bookcases,
and was a long while rummaging about among
the musty books. I found many curious things
I had not noticed before : *Candide*, in a manu-
script translation of somewhere about 1770 ;
newspapers and magazines of the same period ;
the Triumphant Chameleon (that is, Mirabeau),
le Paysan Perverti, etc. I came across children's
books, my own, and my father's, and my grandmother's, and even, fancy, my great grandmother's ; in one dilapidated French grammar
in a particoloured binding, was written in fat
letters : 'Ce livre appartient à Mlle Eudoxie de
Lavrine,' and it was dated 1741. I saw books
I had brought at different times from abroad,
among others, Goethe's *Faust*. You're not
aware, perhaps, that there was a time when I
knew *Faust* by heart (the first part, of course)

word for word ; I was never tired of reading it.
. . But other days, other dreams, and for the
last nine years, it has so happened, that I have
scarcely had a Goethe in my hand. It was
with an indescribable emotion that I saw the
little book I knew so well, again (a poor edition
of 1828). I brought it away with me, lay down
on the bed, and began to read. How all that
splendid first scene affected me ! The entrance
of the Spirit of the Earth, the words, you
remember—'on the tide of life, in the whirl of
creation,' stirred a long unfamiliar tremor and
shiver of ecstasy. I recalled everything : Berlin, and student days, and Fräulein Clara Stick,
and Zeidelmann in the *rôle* of Mephistopheles,
and the music of Radzivil, and all and everything. . . . It was a long while before I could
get to sleep : my youth rose up and stood
before me like a phantom ; it ran like fire, like
poison through my veins, my heart leaped and
would not be still, something plucked at its
chords, and yearnings began surging up. . . .

You see what fantasies your friend gives
himself up to, at almost forty, when he sits in
solitude in his solitary little house ! What if
any one could have peeped at me ! Well,
what ? I shouldn't have been a bit ashamed
of myself. To be ashamed is a sign of youth,
too ; and I have begun (do you know how ?)
to notice that I 'm getting old. I 'll tell you
how. I try in these days to make as much as

I can of my happy sensations, and to make little of my sad ones, and in the days of my youth I did just the opposite. At times, one used to carry about one's melancholy as if it were a treasure, and be ashamed of a cheerful mood . . . But for all that, it strikes me, that in spite of all my experience of life, there is something in the world, friend Horatio, which I have not experienced, and that 'something' almost the most important.

Oh, what have I worked myself up to! Farewell for the present! What are you about in Petersburg? By the way; Savely, my country cook, wishes to send his duty to you. He too is older, but not very much so, he is grown rather corpulent, stouter all over. He is as good as ever at chicken-soup, with stewed onions, cheesecakes with goffered edges, and peagoose—peagoose is the famous dish of the steppes, which makes your tongue white and rough for twenty-four hours after. On the other hand, he roasts the meat as he always did, so that you can hammer on the plate with it—hard as a board. But I must really say, good-bye! Yours,   P. B.

SECOND LETTER

From the SAME to the SAME

M—— VILLAGE, *June* 12, 1850.

I HAVE rather an important piece of news to
tell you, my dear friend. Listen! Yesterday
I felt disposed for a walk before dinner—only
not in the garden; I walked along the road
towards the town. Walking rapidly, quite
aimlessly, along a straight, long road is very
pleasant. You feel as if you're doing something, hurrying somewhere. I look up; a
coach is coming towards me. Surely not some
one to see me, I wondered with secret terror . . .
No: there was a gentleman with moustaches in
the carriage, a stranger to me. I felt reassured.
But all of a sudden, when he got abreast with
me, this gentleman told the coachman to stop
the horses, politely raised his cap, and still
more politely asked me, 'was not I' . . .
mentioning my name. I too came to a standstill, and with the fortitude of a prisoner
brought up for trial, replied that I was myself;
while I stared like a sheep at the gentleman

with the moustaches and said to myself—'I do believe I 've seen him somewhere!'

'You don't recognise me?' he observed, as he got out of the coach.

'No, I don't.'

'But I knew you directly.'

Explanations followed; it appeared that it was Priemkov—do you remember?—a fellow we used to know at the university. 'Why, is that an important piece of news?' you are asking yourself at this instant, my dear Semyon Nikolaitch. 'Priemkov, to the best of my recollection, was rather a dull chap; no harm in him though, and not a fool.' Just so, my dear boy; but hear the rest of our conversation.

'I was delighted,' says he, 'when I heard you had come to your country-place, into our neighbourhood. But I was not alone in that feeling.'

'Allow me to ask,' I questioned: 'who was so kind . . .'

'My wife.'

'Your wife!'

'Yes, my wife; she is an old acquaintance of yours.'

'May I ask what was your wife's name?'

'Vera Nikolaevna; she was an Eltsov . . .'

'Vera Nikolaevna!' I could not help exclaiming . . .

This it is, which is the important piece of news I spoke of at the beginning of my letter.

But perhaps you don't see anything important even in this . . . I shall have to tell you
something of my past . . . long past, life.

When we both left the university in 183—
I was three-and-twenty. You went into the
service; I decided, as you know, to go to
Berlin. But there was nothing to be done in
Berlin before October. I wanted to spend the
summer in Russia—in the country—to have a
good lazy holiday for the last time; and then
to set to work in earnest. How far this last
project was carried out, there is no need to
enlarge upon here . . . 'But where am I to
spend the summer?' I asked myself. I did
not want to go to my own place; my father
had died not long before, I had no near
relations, I was afraid of the solitude and
dreariness . . . And so I was delighted to
receive an invitation from a distant cousin to
stay at his country-place in T . . . province.
He was a well-to-do, good-natured, simple-
hearted man; he lived in style as a country
magnate, and had a palatial country house.
I went to stay there. My cousin had a large
family; two sons and five daughters. Besides
them, there was always a crowd of people in
his house. Guests were for ever arriving; and
yet it wasn't jolly at all. The days were spent
in noisy entertainments, there was no chance
of being by oneself. Everything was done in
common, every one tried to be entertaining,

to invent some amusement, and at the end of
the day every one was fearfully exhausted.
There was something vulgar about the way
we lived. I was already beginning to look
forward to getting away, and was only waiting
till my cousin's birthday festivities were over,
when on the very day of those festivities, at
the ball, I saw Vera Nikolaevna Eltsov—and I
stayed on.

She was at that time sixteen. She was
living with her mother on a little estate four
miles from my cousin's place. Her father—a
remarkable man, I have been told—had risen
rapidly to the grade of colonel, and would
have attained further distinctions, but he died
young, accidentally shot by a friend when out
shooting. Vera Nikolaevna was a baby at
the time of his death. Her mother too was
an exceptional woman; she spoke several
languages, and was very well informed. She
was seven or eight years older than her husband
whom she had married for love; he had run
away with her in secret from her father's house.
She never got over his loss, and, till the day of
her death (I heard from Priemkov that she had
died soon after her daughter's marriage), she
never wore anything but black. I have a vivid
recollection of her face: it was expressive, dark,
with thick hair beginning to turn grey; large,
severe, lustreless eyes, and a straight, fine nose.
Her father—his surname was Ladanov—had

lived for fifteen years in Italy. Vera Nikolaevna's mother was the daughter of a simple
Albanian peasant girl, who, the day after
giving birth to her child, was killed by her
betrothed lover—a Transteverino peasant—
from whom Ladanov had enticed her away.
. . . The story made a great sensation at the
time. On his return to Russia, Ladanov never
left his house, nor even his study ; he devoted
himself to chemistry, anatomy, and magical
arts; tried to discover means to prolong
human life, fancied he could hold intercourse
with spirits, and call up the dead. . . . The
neighbours looked upon him as a sorcerer.
He was extremely fond of his daughter, and
taught her everything himself: but he never
forgave her elopement with Eltsov, never
allowed either of them to come into his
presence, predicted a life of sorrow for both
of them, and died in solitude. When Madame
Eltsov was left a widow, she devoted her whole
time to the education of her daughter, and
scarcely saw any friends. When I first met
Vera Nikolaevna, she had—just fancy—never
been in a town in her life, not even in the
town of her district.

Vera Nikolaevna was not like the common
run of Russian girls ; there was the stamp of
something special upon her. I was struck
from the first minute by the extraordinary
repose of all her movements and remarks.

She seemed free from any sort of disturbance or agitation ; she answered simply and intelligently, and listened attentively. The expression of her face was sincere and truthful as a child's, but a little cold and immobile, though not dreamy. She was rarely gay, and not in the way other girls are; the serenity of an innocent heart shone out in everything about her, and cheered one more than any gaiety. She was not tall, and had a very good figure, rather slender ; she had soft, regular features, a lovely smooth brow, light golden hair, a straight nose, like her mother's, and rather full lips ; her dark grey eyes looked out somewhat too directly from under soft, upward-turned eyelashes. Her hands were small, and not very pretty ; one never sees hands like hers on people of talent . . . and, as a fact, Vera Nikolaevna had no special talents. Her voice rang out clear as a child of seven's. I was presented to her mother at my cousin's ball, and a few days later I called on them for the first time.

Madame Eltsov was a very strange woman, a woman of character, of strong will and concentration. She had a great influence on me ; I at once respected her and feared her. Everything with her was done on a principle, and she had educated her daughter too on a principle, though she did not interfere with her freedom. Her daughter loved her and trusted her blindly. Madame Eltsov had only to give her a book, and say—'Don't read that page,' she would prefer to skip the preceding page as well, and would certainly never glance at the page interdicted. But Madame Eltsov too had her *idées fixes*, her fads. She was mortally afraid, for instance, of anything that might work upon the imagination. And so her daughter reached the age of seventeen without ever having read a novel or a poem, while in Geography, History, and even Natural History, she would often put me to shame, graduate as I was, and a graduate, as you know, not by any means low down on the list either. I used to try and argue with Madame Eltsov about her fad, though it was difficult to draw her into conversation; she was very silent. She simply shook her head.

'You tell me,' she said at last, 'that reading poetry is *both* useful *and* pleasant. . . . I consider one must make one's choice early in life; *either* the useful *or* the pleasant, and abide by it once for all. I, too, tried at one time to unite the two. . . . That's impossible, and leads to ruin or vulgarity.'

Yes, a wonderful being she was, that woman, an upright, proud nature, not without a certain fanaticism and superstition of her own. 'I am afraid of life,' she said to me one day. And really she was afraid of it, afraid of those secret forces on which life rests and which rarely, but so suddenly, break out. Woe to him who is their sport! These forces had shown themselves in fearful shape for Madame Eltsov; think of her mother's death, her husband's, her father's. . . . Any one would have been panic-stricken. I never saw her smile. She had, as it were, locked herself up and thrown the key into the water. She must have suffered great grief in her time, and had never shared it with any one; she had hidden it all away within herself. She had so thoroughly trained herself not to give way to her feelings that she was even ashamed to express her passionate love for her daughter; she never once kissed her in my presence, and never used any endearing names, always Vera. I remember one saying of hers; I happened to say to her that all of us modern people were half broken by life. 'It's no good being half broken,' she observed; 'one must be broken in thoroughly or let it alone. . . .'

Very few people visited Madame Eltsov; but I went often to see her. I was secretly aware that she looked on me with favour; and I liked Vera Nikolaevna very much indeed. We used to talk and walk together. . . . Her mother was no check upon us; the daughter did not like to be away from her mother, and I, for my part, felt no craving for solitary talks with her. . . . Vera Nikolaevna had a strange habit of thinking aloud; she used at night in her sleep to talk loudly and distinctly about what had impressed her during the day. One day, looking at me attentively, leaning softly, as her way was, on her hand, she said, 'It seems to me that B. is a good person, but there's no relying on him.' The relations existing between us were of the friendliest and most tranquil ; only once I fancied I detected somewhere far off in the very depths of her clear eyes something strange, a sort of softness and tenderness. . . . But perhaps I was mistaken.

Meanwhile the time was slipping by, and it was already time for me to prepare for departure. But still I put it off. At times, when I thought, when I realised that soon I should see no more of this sweet girl I had grown so fond of, I felt sick at heart. . . . Berlin began to lose its attractive force. I had not the courage to acknowledge to myself what was going on within me, and, indeed, I didn't understand what was taking place,—it was as though a cloud were overhanging my soul. At last one morning everything suddenly became clear to me. 'Why seek further, what is there to strive towards? Why, I shall not attain to truth in any case. Isn't it better to stay here, to be married ? ' And, imagine, the idea of marriage had no terrors for me in those days. On the contrary, I rejoiced in it. More than that ; that day I declared my intentions ; only not to Vera Nikolaevna, as one would

naturally suppose, but to Madame Eltsov.
The old lady looked at me.

'No,' she said; 'my dear boy, go to Berlin,
get broken in thoroughly. You're a good
fellow; but it's not a husband like you that's
needed for Vera.'

I hung my head, blushed, and, what will
very likely surprise you still more, inwardly
agreed with Madame Eltsov on the spot. A
week later I went away, and since then I have
not seen her nor Vera Nikolaevna.

I have related this episode briefly because I
know you don't care for anything 'meandering.'
When I got to Berlin I very quickly forgot
Vera Nikolaevna. . . . But I will own that
hearing of her so unexpectedly has excited me.
I am impressed by the idea that she is so close,
that she is my neighbour, that I shall see her
in a day or two. The past seems suddenly to
have sprung up out of the earth before my
eyes, and to have rushed down upon me.
Priemkov informed me that he was coming to
call upon me with the very object of renewing
our old acquaintance, and that he should look
forward to seeing me at his house as soon
as I could possibly come. He told me he
had been in the cavalry, had retired with the
rank of lieutenant, had bought an estate
about six miles from me, and was intending
to devote himself to its management, that
he had had three children, but that two had

died, and he had only a little girl of five surviving.

'And does your wife remember me?' I inquired.

'Yes, she remembers you,' he replied, with some slight hesitation. 'Of course, she was a child, one may say, in those days; but her mother always spoke very highly of you, and you know how precious every word of her poor mother's is to her.'

I recalled Madame Eltsov's words, that I was not suitable for her Vera. . . . 'I suppose *you* were suitable,' I thought, with a sidelong look at Priemkov. He spent some hours with me. He is a very nice, dear, good fellow, speaks so modestly, and looks at me so good-naturedly. One can't help liking him . . . but his intellectual powers have not developed since we used to know him. I shall certainly go and see him, possibly to-morrow. I am exceedingly curious to see how Vera Nikolaevna has turned out.

You, spiteful fellow, are most likely laughing at me as you read this, sitting at your directors' table. But I shall write and tell you, all the same, the impression she makes on me. Good-bye—till my next.—Yours,   P. B.

THIRD LETTER

From the SAME to the SAME

M—— VILLAGE, *June* 16, 1850.

WELL, my dear boy, I have been to her house; I have seen her. First of all I must tell you one astonishing fact: you may believe me or not as you like, but she has scarcely changed at all either in face or in figure. When she came to meet me, I almost cried out in amazement; it was simply a little girl of seventeen! Only her eyes are not a little girl's; but then her eyes were never like a child's, even in her young days,—they were too clear. But the same composure, the same serenity, the same voice, not one line on her brow, as though she had been laid in the snow all these years. And she's twenty-eight now, and has had three children. . . . It's incomprehensible! Don't imagine, please, that I had some preconceived preference, and so am exaggerating; quite the other way; I don't like this absence of change in her a bit.

A woman of eight-and-twenty, a wife and a

mother, ought not to be like a little girl; she should have gained something from life. She gave me a very cordial welcome; but Priemkov was simply overjoyed at my arrival; the dear fellow seems on the look-out for some one to make much of. Their house is very cosy and clean. Vera Nikolaevna was dressed, too, like a girl; all in white, with a blue sash, and a slender gold chain on her neck. Her daughter is very sweet and not at all like her. She reminds one of her grandmother. In the drawing-room, just over a sofa, there hangs a portrait of that strange woman, a striking likeness. It caught my eye directly I went into the room. It seemed as though she were gazing sternly and earnestly at me. We sat down, spoke of old times, and by degrees got into conversation. I could not help continually glancing at the gloomy portrait of Madame Eltsov. Vera Nikolaevna was sitting just under it; it is her favourite place. Imagine my amazement: Vera Nikolaevna has never yet read a single novel, a single poem—in fact, not a single invented work, as she expresses it! This incomprehensible indifference to the highest pleasures of the intellect irritated me. In a woman of intelligence, and as far as I can judge, of sensibility, it's simply unpardonable.

'What? do you make it a principle,' I asked, 'never to read books of that sort?'

'I have never happened to,' she answered; 'I haven't had time!'

'Not time! You surprise me! I should have thought,' I went on, addressing Priemkov, 'you would have interested your wife in poetry.'

'I should have been delighted——' Priemkov was beginning, but Vera Nikolaevna interrupted him—

'Don't pretend; you've no great love for poetry yourself.'

'Poetry; well, no,' he began; 'I'm not very fond of it; but novels, now. . . .'

'But what do **you** do, how do **you** spend **your** evenings?' I queried; 'do you play cards?'

'We sometimes play,' she answered; 'but there's always plenty to do. We read, too; there are good books to read besides poetry.'

'Why are you so set against poetry?'

'I'm not set against it; I have been used to not reading these invented works from a child. That was my mother's wish, and the longer I live the more I am convinced that everything my mother did, everything she said, was right, sacredly right.'

'Well, as you will, but I can't agree with you; I am certain you are depriving yourself quite needlessly of the purest, the most legitimate pleasure. Why, you're not opposed to music and painting, I suppose; why be opposed to poetry?'

'I'm not opposed to it; I have never got to know anything of it—that's all.'

'Well, then, I will see to that! Your mother did not, I suppose, wish to prevent your knowing anything of the works of creative, poetic art all your life?'

'No; when I was married, my mother removed every restriction; it never occurred to me to read—what did you call them? . . . well, anyway, to read novels.'

I listened to Vera Nikolaevna in astonishment. I had not expected this.

She looked at me with her serene glance. Birds look so when they are not frightened.

'I'll bring you a book!' I cried. (I thought of *Faust*, which I had just been reading.)

Vera Nikolaevna gave a gentle sigh.

'It——it won't be Georges—Sand?' she questioned with some timidity.

'Ah! then you've heard of her? Well, if it were, where's the harm? . . . No, I'll bring you another author. You've not forgotten German, have you?'

'No.'

'She speaks it like a German,' put in Priemkov.

'Well, that's splendid! I will bring you—but there, you shall see what a wonderful thing I will bring you.'

'Very good, we shall see. But now let us

go into the garden, or there'll be no keeping Natasha still.'

She put on a round straw hat, a child's hat, just such a one as her daughter was wearing, only a little larger, and we went into the garden. I walked beside her. In the fresh air, in the shade of the tall limes, I thought her face looked sweeter than ever, especially when she turned a little and threw back her head so as to look up at me from under the brim of her hat. If it had not been for Priemkov walking behind us, and the little girl skipping about in front of us, I could really have fancied I was three-and-twenty, instead of thirty-five ; and that I was just on the point of starting for Berlin, especially as the garden we were walking in was very much like the garden in Madame Eltsov's estate. I could not help expressing my feelings to Vera Nikolaevna.

'Every one tells me that I am very little changed externally,' she answered, 'though indeed I have remained just the same inwardly too.'

We came up to a little Chinese summer-house.

'We had no summer-house like this at Osinovka,' she said ; 'but you mustn't mind its being so tumbledown and discoloured : it's very nice and cool inside.'

We went into the house. I looked round.

'I tell you what, Vera Nikolaevna,' I observed, 'you let them bring a table and some chairs in here. Here it is really delicious. I will read you here Goethe's *Faust*—that's the thing I am going to read you.'

'Yes, there are no flies here,' she observed simply. 'When will you come?'

'The day after to-morrow.'

'Very well,' she answered. 'I will arrange it.'

Natasha, who had come into the summer-house with us, suddenly gave a shriek and jumped back, quite pale.

'What is it?' inquired Vera Nikolaevna.

'O mammy,' said the little girl, pointing into the corner, 'look, what a dreadful spider!'

Vera Nikolaevna looked into the corner: a fat mottled spider was crawling slowly along the wall.

'What is there to fear in that?' she said. 'It won't bite, look.'

And before I had time to stop her, she took up the hideous insect, let it run over her hand, and threw it away.

'Well, you are brave!' I cried.

'Where is the bravery in that? It wasn't a venomous spider.'

'One can see you are as well up in Natural History as ever, but I couldn't have held it in my hand.'

'There's nothing to be afraid of!' repeated Vera Nikolaevna.

Natasha looked at us both in silence, and laughed.

'How like your mother she is!' I remarked.

'Yes,' rejoined Vera Nikolaevna with a smile of pleasure, 'it is a great happiness to me. God grant she may be like her, not in face only!'

We were called in to dinner, and after dinner I went away.

N.B.—The dinner was very good and well-cooked, an observation in parenthesis for you, you gourmand!

To-morrow I shall take them *Faust.* I'm afraid old Goethe and I may not come off very well. I will write and tell you all about it most exactly.

Well, and what do you think of all these proceedings? No doubt, that she has made a great impression on me, that I'm on the point of falling in love, and all the rest of it? Rubbish, my dear boy! There's a limit to everything. I've been fool enough. No more! One can't begin life over again at my age. Besides, I never did care for women of that sort. . . . Nice sort of women I did care for, if you come to that!!

'I shudder—my heart is sick—
I am ashamed of my idols.'

Any way, I am very glad of such neighbours, glad of the opportunity of seeing something of an intelligent, simple, bright creature. And as to what comes of it later on, you shall hear in due time.—Yours,   P. B.

FOURTH LETTER

From the SAME to the SAME

THE reading took place yesterday, dear friend,
and here follows the manner thereof. First of
all, I hasten to tell you : a success quite beyond
all expectation—success, in fact, is not the word.
. . . Well, I'll tell you. I arrived to dinner.
We sat down a party of six to dinner : she,
Priemkov, their little girl, the governess (an
uninteresting colourless figure), I, and an old
German in a short cinnamon-coloured frock-coat,
very clean, well-shaved and brushed ; he had the
meekest, most honest face, and a toothless
smile, and smelled of coffee mixed with chicory
. . . all old Germans have that peculiar odour
about them. I was introduced to him ; he was
one Schimmel, a German tutor, living with
the princes H., neighbours of the Priemkovs.
Vera Nikolaevna, it appeared, had a liking for
him, and had invited him to be present at the
reading. We dined late, and sat a long while
at table, and afterwards went a walk. The

weather was exquisite. In the morning there had been rain and a blustering wind, but towards evening all was calm again. We came out on to an open meadow. Directly over the meadow a great rosy cloud poised lightly, high up in the sky; streaks of grey stretched like smoke over it; on its very edge, continually peeping out and vanishing again, quivered a little star, while a little further off the crescent of the moon shone white upon a background of azure, faintly flushed with red. I drew Vera Nikolaevna's attention to the cloud.

'Yes,' she said, 'that is lovely; but look in this direction.' I looked round. An immense dark-blue storm-cloud rose up, hiding the setting sun; it reared a crest like a thick sheaf flung upwards against the sky; it was surrounded by a bright rim of menacing purple, which in one place, in the very middle, broke right through its mighty mass, like fire from a burning crater. . . .

'There'll be a storm,' remarked Priemkov.

But I am wandering from the main point.

I forgot to tell you in my last letter that when I got home from the Priemkovs' I felt sorry I had mentioned *Faust*; Schiller would have been a great deal better for the first time, if it was to be something German. I felt especially afraid of the first scenes, before the meeting with Gretchen. I was not quite easy

about Mephistopheles either. But I was under
t.e spell of *Faust*, and there was nothing else
I could have read with zest. It was quite dark
when we went into the summer-house; it had
been made ready for us the day before. Just
opposite the door, before a little sofa, stood a
round table covered with a cloth; easy-chairs
and seats were placed round it; there was a
lamp alight on the table. I sat down on the little
sofa, and took out the book. Vera Nikolaevna
settled herself in an easy-chair, a little way off,
close to the door. In the darkness, through
the door, a green branch of acacia stood out
in the lamplight, swaying lightly; from time
to time a flood of night air flowed into the
room. Priemkov sat near me at the table, the
German beside him. The governess had remained in the house with Natasha. I made
a brief, introductory speech. I touched on the
old legend of doctor Faust, the significance of
Mephistopheles, and Goethe himself, and asked
them to stop me if anything struck them as
obscure. Then I cleared my throat. . . .
Priemkov asked me if I wouldn't have some
sugar water, and one could perceive that he
was very well satisfied with himself for having
put this question to me. I refused. Profound
silence reigned. I began to read, without raising
my eyes. I felt ill at ease; my heart beat,
and my voice shook. The first exclamation
of sympathy came from the German, and he

was the only one to break the silence all
the while I was reading. . . . 'Wonderful!
sublime!' he repeated, adding now and then,
'Ah! that's profound.' Priemkov, as far as I
could observe, was bored; he did not know
German very well, and had himself admitted
he did not care for poetry! . . . Well, it was
his own doing! I had wanted to hint at dinner
that his company could be dispensed with at
the reading, but I felt a delicacy about saying
so. Vera Nikolaevna did not stir; twice I stole
a glance at her. Her eyes were fixed directly
and intently upon me; her face struck me as
pale. After the first meeting of Faust with
Gretchen she bent forward in her low chair,
clasped her hands, and remained motionless in
that position till the end. I felt that Priemkov
was thoroughly sick of it, and at first that depressed me, but gradually I forgot him, warmed
up, and read with fire, with enthusiasm. . . . I
was reading for Vera Nikolaevna alone; an
inner voice told me that *Faust* was affect-
ing her. When I finished (the intermezzo I
omitted: that bit belongs in style to the second
part, and I skipped part, too, of the 'Night
on the Brocken') . . . when I finished, when
that last 'Heinrich!' was heard, the German
with much feeling commented—'My God! how
splendid!' Priemkov, apparently overjoyed
(poor chap!), leaped up, gave a sigh, and began
thanking me for the treat I had given them

... But I made him no reply; I looked towards Vera Nikolaevna. . . . I wanted to hear what she would say. She got up, walked irresolutely towards the door, stood a moment in the doorway, and softly went out into the garden. I rushed after her. She was already some paces off; her dress was just visible, a white patch in the thick shadow.

'Well?' I called—'didn't you like it?'

She stopped.

'Can you leave me that book?' I heard her voice saying.

'I will present it you, Vera Nikolaevna, if you care to have it.'

'Thank you!' she answered, and disappeared.

Priemkov and the German came up to me.

'How wonderfully warm it is!' observed Priemkov; 'it's positively stifling. But where has my wife gone?'

'Home, I think,' I answered.

'I suppose it will soon be time for supper,' he rejoined. 'You read splendidly,' he added, after a short pause.

'Vera Nikolaevna liked *Faust*, I think,' said I.

'No doubt of it!' cried Priemkov.

'Oh, of course!' chimed in Schimmel.

We went into the house.

'Where's your mistress?' Priemkov inquired of a maid who happened to meet us.

'She has gone to her bedroom.'

Priemkov went off to her bedroom.

I went out on to the terrace with Schimmel. The old man raised his eyes towards the sky.

'How many stars!' he said slowly, taking a pinch of snuff; 'and all are worlds,' he added, and he took another pinch.

I did not feel it necessary to answer him, and simply gazed upwards in silence. A secret uncertainty weighed upon my heart. . . . The stars, I fancied, looked down seriously at us. Five minutes later Priemkov appeared and called us into the dining-room. Vera Nikolaevna came in soon after. We sat down.

'Look at Verotchka,' Priemkov said to me.

I glanced at her.

'Well? don't you notice anything?'

I certainly did notice a change in her face, but I answered, I don't know why—

'No, nothing.'

'Her eyes are red,' Priemkov went on.

I was silent.

'Only fancy! I went upstairs to her and found her crying. It's a long while since such a thing has happened to her. I can tell you the last time she cried; it was when our Sasha died. You see what you have done with your *Faust*!' he added, with a smile.

'So you see now, Vera Nikolaevna,' I began, 'that I was right when——'

'I did not expect this,' she interrupted me; 'but God knows whether you are right. Perhaps that was the very reason my mother forbade my reading such books,—she knew——'

Vera Nikolaevna stopped.

'What did she know?' I asked. 'Tell me.'

'What for? I'm ashamed of myself, as it is; what did I cry for? But we'll talk about it another time. There was a great deal I did not quite understand.'

'Why didn't you stop me?'

'I understood all the words, and the meaning of them, but——'

She did not finish her sentence, and looked away dreamily. At that instant there came from the garden the sound of rustling leaves, suddenly fluttering in the rising wind. Vera Nikolaevna started and looked round towards the open window.

'I told you there would be a storm!' cried Priemkov. 'But what made you start like that, Verotchka?'

She glanced at him without speaking. A faint, far-off flash of lightning threw a mysterious light on her motionless face.

'It's all due to your *Faust*,' Priemkov went on. 'After supper we must all go to by-by. . . . Mustn't we, Herr Schimmel?'

'After intellectual enjoyment physical repose is as grateful as it is beneficial,' responded the kind-hearted German, and he drank a wine-glass of vodka.

Immediately after supper we separated. As

I said good-night to Vera Nikolaevna I pressed
her hand ; her hand was cold.   I went up to
the room assigned to me, and stood a long
while at the window before I undressed and
got into bed.   Priemkov's prediction was ful-
filled ; the storm came close, and broke.   I
listened to the roar of the wind, the patter and
splash of the rain, and watched how the church,
built close by, above the lake, at each flash of
lightning stood out, at one moment black
against a background of white, at the next
white against a background of black, and then
was swallowed up in the darkness again. . . .
But my thoughts were far away.   I kept
thinking of Vera Nikolaevna, of what she
would say to me when she had read *Faust*
herself, I thought of her tears, remembered
how she had listened. . . .

The storm had long passed away, the stars
came out, all was hushed around.   Some bird
I did not know sang different notes, several
times in succession repeating the same phrase.
Its clear, solitary voice rang out strangely in
the deep stillness ; and still I did not go to
bed. . . .

Next morning, earlier than all the rest, I
was down in the drawing-room.   I stood before
the portrait of Madame Eltsov.   'Aha,' I
thought, with a secret feeling of ironical tri-
umph, ' after all, I have read your daughter a
forbidden book ! '   All at once I fancied—you

have most likely noticed that eyes *en face* always seem fixed straight on any one looking at a picture—but this time I positively fancied the old lady moved them with a reproachful look on me.

I turned round, went to the window, and caught sight of Vera Nikolaevna. With a parasol on her shoulder and a light white kerchief on her head, she was walking about the garden. I went out at once and said good-morning to her.

' I didn't sleep all night,' she said; ' my head aches; I came out into the air—it may go off.'

'Can that be the result of yesterday's reading?' I asked.

'Of course; I am not used to it. There are things in your book I can't get out of my mind; I feel as though they were simply turning my head,' she added, putting her hand to her forehead.

'That's splendid,' I commented; 'but I tell you what I don't like—I'm afraid this sleeplessness and headache may turn you against reading such things.'

'You think so?' she responded, and she picked a sprig of wild jasmine as she passed. 'God knows! I fancy if one has once entered on that path, there is no turning back.'

She suddenly flung away the spray.

'Come, let us sit down in this arbour,' she went on; 'and please, until I talk of it of my

own accord, don't remind me—of that book.'
(She seemed afraid to utter the name *Faust*.)

We went into the arbour and sat down.

'I won't talk to you about *Faust*,' I began ;
'but you will let me congratulate you and tell
you that I envy you.'

'You envy me?'

'Yes ; you, as I know you now, with your
soul, have such delights awaiting you! There
are great poets besides Goethe ; Shakespeare,
Schiller—and, indeed, our own Pushkin, and
you must get to know him too.'

She did not speak, and drew in the sand
with her parasol.

O, my friend, Semyon Nikolaitch ! if you
could have seen how sweet she was at that
instant ; pale almost to transparency, stooping
forward a little, weary, inwardly perturbed—and
yet serene as the sky! I talked, talked a long
while, then ceased, and sat in silence watching
her. . . . She did not raise her eyes, and went
on drawing with her parasol and rubbing it out
again. Suddenly we heard quick, childish steps;
Natasha ran into the arbour. Vera Nikolaevna
drew herself up, rose, and to my surprise she
embraced her daughter with a sort of passionate
tenderness. . . . That was not one of her ways.
Then Priemkov made his appearance. Schimmel, that grey-haired but punctual innocent,
had left before daybreak so as not to miss a
lesson. We went in to morning tea.

But I am tired; it's high time to finish this letter. It's sure to strike you as foolish and confused. I feel confused myself. I'm not myself. I don't know what's the matter with me. I am continually haunted by a little room with bare walls, a lamp, an open door, the fragrance and freshness of the night, and there, near the door, an intent youthful face, light white garments. . . . I understand now why I wanted to marry her: I was not so stupid, it seems, before my stay in Berlin as I had hitherto supposed. Yes, Semyon Nikolaitch, your friend is in a curious frame of mind. All this I know will pass off . . . and if it doesn't pass off,—well, what then? it won't pass off, and that's all. But any way I am well satisfied with myself; in the first place, I have spent an exquisite evening; and secondly, if I have awakened that soul, who can blame me? Old Madame Eltsov is nailed up on the wall, and must hold her peace. The old thing! . . . I don't know all the details of her life; but I know she ran away from her father's house; she was not half Italian for nothing, it seems. She wanted to keep her daughter secure . . . we shall see.

I must put down my pen. You, jeering person, pray think what you like of me, only don't jeer at me in writing. You and I are old friends, and ought to spare each other. Good-bye!—Yours,   P. B.

FIFTH LETTER

From the SAME to the SAME

M—— VILLAGE, *July* 26, 1850.

IT's a long time since I wrote to you, dear
Semyon Nicolaitch ; more than a month, I
think.   I had enough to write about but I was
overcome by laziness.   To tell the truth, I
have hardly thought of you all this time.   But
from your last letter to me I gather that you
are drawing conclusions in regard to me, which
are unjust, that is to say, not altogether just.
You imagine I have fallen in love with Vera
(I feel it awkward, somehow, to call her Vera
Nikolaevna) ; you are wrong.   Of course I see
her often, I like her extremely . . . indeed,
who wouldn't like her ?   I should like to see
you in my place.   She's an exquisite creature !
Rapid intuition, together with the inexperience
of a child, clear common-sense, and an innate
feeling for beauty, a continual striving towards
the true and the lofty, and a comprehension
of everything, even of the vicious, even of
the ridiculous, a soft womanly charm brooding

FAUST

over all this like an angel's white wings . . .
But what's the use of words! We have read
a great deal, we have talked a great deal
together during this month. Reading with
her is a delight such as I had never experienced before. You seem to be discovering new
worlds. She never goes into ecstasies over
anything; anything boisterous is distasteful to
her; she is softly radiant all over when she
likes anything, and her face wears such a
noble and good—yes, good expression. From
her earliest childhood Vera has not known
what deceit was; she is accustomed to truth,
it is the breath of her being, and so in poetry
too, only what is true strikes her as natural;
at once, without effort or difficulty, she recog-
nises it as a familiar face . . . a great privilege
and happiness. One must give her mother
credit for it. How many times have I thought,
as I watched Vera—yes, Goethe was right,
'the good even in their obscure striving feel
always where the true path lies.' There is
only one thing annoying—her husband is
always about the place. (Please don't laugh
a senseless guffaw, don't sully our pure friendship, even in thought). He is about as capable
of understanding poetry as I am of playing the
flute, but he does not like to lag behind his
wife, he wants to improve himself too. Sometimes she puts me out of patience herself; all
of a sudden a mood comes over her; she won't

read or talk, she works at her embroidery frame, busies herself with Natasha, or with the housekeeper, runs off all at once into the kitchen, or simply sits with her hands folded looking out of the window, or sets to playing 'fools' with the nurse ... I have noticed at these times it doesn't do to bother her; it's better to bide one's time till she comes up, begins to talk or takes up a book. She has a great deal of independence, and I am very glad of it. In the days of our youth, do you remember, young girls would sometimes repeat one's own words to one, as they so well knew how, and one would be in ecstasies over the echo, and possibly quite impressed by it, till one realised what it meant? but this woman's ... not so; she thinks for herself. She takes nothing on trust; there's no overawing her with authority; she won't begin arguing; but she won't give in either. We have discussed *Faust* more than once; but, strange to say, Gretchen she never speaks of, herself, she only listens to what I say of her. Mephistopheles terrifies her, not as the devil, but as 'something which may exist in every man.' ... These are her own words. I began trying to convince her that this 'something' is what we call reflection; but she does not understand the word reflection in its German sense; she only knows the French 'refléxion,' and is accustomed to regarding it as useful. Our relations are marvellous! From a certain point of view I can say that I have a great influence over her, and am, as it were, educating her; but she too, though she is unaware of it herself, is changing me for the better in many ways. It's only lately, for instance—thanks to her—that I have discovered what an immense amount of conventional, rhetorical stuff there is in many fine and celebrated poetical works. What leaves her cold is at once suspect in my eyes. Yes, I have grown better, serener. One can't be near her, see her, and remain the man one was.

What will come of all this? you ask. I really believe—nothing. I shall pass my time very delightfully till September and then go away. Life will seem dark and dreary to me for the first months . . . I shall get used to it. I know how full of danger is any tie whatever between a man and a young woman, how imperceptibly one feeling passes into another . . . I should have had the strength to break it off, if I had not been sure that we were both perfectly undisturbed. It is true one day something queer passed between us. I don't know how or from what—I remember we had been reading *Oniegin*—I kissed her hand. She turned a little away, bent her eyes upon me (I have never seen such a look, except in her; there is dreaminess and intent attention in it, and a sort of sternness), . . . suddenly

flushed, got up and went away. I did not
succeed in being alone with her that day. She
avoided me, and for four mortal hours she
played cards with her husband, the nurse, and
the governess! Next morning she proposed
a walk in the garden to me. We walked all
through it, down to the lake. Suddenly without turning towards me, she softly whispered—
'Please don't do that again!' and instantly
began telling me about something else. . . .
I was very much ashamed.

I must admit that her image is never out of
my mind, and indeed I may almost say I have
begun writing a letter to you with the object
of having a reason for thinking and talking
about her. I hear the tramp and neighing of
horses; it's my carriage being got ready. I
am going to see them. My coachman has
given up asking me where to drive to, when
I get into my carriage—he takes me straight
off to the Priemkovs'. A mile and a half from
their village, at an abrupt turn in the road,
their house suddenly peeps out from behind
a birch copse . . . Each time I feel a thrill of
joy in my heart directly I catch the glimmer
of its windows in the distance. Schimmel (the
harmless old man comes to see them from
time to time; the princes H——, thank God,
have only called once) . . . Schimmel, with
the modest solemnity characteristic of him,
said very aptly, pointing to the house where

Vera lives: 'That is the abode of peace!' In that house dwells an angel of peace. . . .

> Cover me with thy wing,
> Still the throbbing of my heart,
> And grateful will be the shade
> To the enraptured soul. . . .

But enough of this; or you'll be fancying all sorts of things. Till next time . . . What shall I write to you next time, I wonder?— Good-bye! By the way, she never says 'Good-bye,' but always, 'So, good-bye!'—I like that tremendously.—Yours, P. B.

P.S.—I can't recollect whether I told you that she knows I wanted to marry her.

SIXTH LETTER

From the SAME to the SAME

M—— VILLAGE, August 10, 1850.

CONFESS you are expecting a letter from me
of despair or of rapture! . . . Nothing of the
sort. My letter will be like any other letter.
Nothing new has happened, and nothing, I
imagine, possibly can happen. The other day
we went out in a boat on the lake. I will tell
you about this boating expedition. We were
three: she, Schimmel, and I. I don't know
what induces her to invite the old fellow so
often. The H——s, I hear, are annoyed with
him for neglecting his lessons. This time,
though, he was entertaining. Priemkov did
not come with us; he had a headache. The
weather was splendid, brilliant; great white
clouds that seemed torn to shreds over a blue
sky, everywhere glitter, a rustle in the trees,
the plash and lapping of water on the bank,
running coils of gold on the waves, freshness
and sunlight! At first the German and I
rowed; then we hoisted a sail and flew before

the wind. The boat's bow almost dipped in the water, and a constant hissing and foaming followed the helm. She sat at the rudder and steered ; she tied a kerchief over her head ; she could not have kept a hat on ; her curls strayed from under it and fluttered in the air. She held the rudder firmly in her little sun-burnt hand, and smiled at the spray which flew at times in her face. I was curled up at the bottom of the boat ; not far from her feet. The German brought out a pipe, smoked his shag, and, only fancy, began singing in a rather pleasing bass. First he sang the old-fashioned song : 'Freut euch des Lebens,' then an air from the 'Magic Flute,' then a song called the 'A B C of Love.' In this song all the letters of the alphabet—with additions of course—are sung through in order, beginning with 'A B C D—Wenn ich dich seh!' and ending with 'U V W X—Mach einen Knicks!' He sang all the couplets with much expression ; but you should have seen how slily he winked with his left eye at the word 'Knicks!' Vera laughed and shook her finger at him. I observed that, as far as I could judge, Mr. Schimmel had been a redoubtable fellow in his day. 'Oh yes, I could take my own part!' he rejoined with dignity; and he knocked the ash out of his pipe on to his open hand, and, with a knowing air, held the mouth-piece on one side in his teeth, while he felt in the tobacco-pouch.

'When I was a student,' he added, 'o-oh-oh!'
He said nothing more.   But what an o-oh-oh!
it was!   Vera begged him to sing some
students' song, and he sang her: 'Knaster, den
gelben,' but broke down on the last note.
Altogether he was quite jovial and expansive.
Meanwhile the wind had blown up, the waves
began to be rather large, and the boat heeled
a little over on one side; swallows began
flitting above the water all about us.   We
made the sail loose and began to tack about.
The wind suddenly blew a cross squall, we had
not time to right the sail, a wave splashed over
the boat's edge and flung a lot of water into
the boat.   And now the German proved himself a man of spirit; he snatched the cord from
me, and set the sail right, saying as he did so—
'So macht man ins Kuxhaven!'

Vera was most likely frightened, for she
turned pale, but as her way is, she did not utter
a word, but picked up her skirt, and put her
feet upon the crosspiece of the boat.   I was
suddenly reminded of the poem of Goethe's (I
have been simply steeped in him for some time
past) . . . you remember?—'On the waves
glitter a thousand dancing stars,' and I repeated
it aloud.   When I reached the line: 'My eyes,
why do you look down?' she slightly raised
her eyes (I was sitting lower than she; her gaze
had rested on me from above) and looked a long
while away into the distance, screwing up her

eyes from the wind. . . . A light rain came on
in an instant, and pattered, making bubbles on
the water. I offered her my overcoat; she put
it over her shoulders. We got to the bank—
not at the landing-place—and walked home. I
gave her my arm. I kept feeling that I wanted
to tell her something; but I did not speak.
I asked her, though, I remember, why she
always sat, when she was at home, under the
portrait of Madame Eltsov, like a little bird
under its mother's wing. 'Your comparison is
a very true one,' she responded, ' I never want
to come out from under her wing.' ' Shouldn't
you like to come out into freedom?' I asked
again. She made no answer.

I don't know why I have described this
expedition—perhaps, because it has remained
in my memory as one of the brightest events
of the past days, though, in reality, how can
one call it an event? I had such a sense of
comfort and unspeakable gladness of heart, and
tears, light, happy tears were on the point of
bursting from my eyes.

Oh! fancy, the next day, as I was walking
in the garden by the arbour, I suddenly heard
a pleasing, musical, woman's voice singing—
'Freut euch des Lebens!' . . . I glanced into the
arbour: it was Vera. 'Bravo!' I cried; 'I
didn't know you had such a splendid voice.'
She was rather abashed, and did not speak.
Joking apart, she has a fine, strong soprano.

And I do believe she has never even suspected that she has a good voice. What treasures of untouched wealth lie hid in her! She does not know herself. But am I not right in saying such a woman is a rarity in our time?

August 12.

We had a very strange conversation yesterday. We touched first upon apparitions. Fancy, she believes in them, and says she has her own reasons for it. Priemkov, who was sitting there, dropped his eyes, and shook his head, as though in confirmation of her words. I began questioning her, but soon noticed that this conversation was disagreeable to her. We began talking of imagination, of the power of imagination. I told them that in my youth I used to dream a great deal about happiness (the common occupation of people, who have not had or are not having good luck in life). Among other dreams, I used to brood over the bliss it would be to spend a few weeks, with the woman I loved, in Venice. I so often mused over this, especially at night, that gradually there grew up in my head a whole picture, which I could call up at will: I had only to close my eyes. This is what I imagined—night, a moon, the moonlight white and soft, a scent—of lemon, do you suppose? no, of vanilla, a scent of cactus, a wide expanse of water, a flat island overgrown with olives; on the island, at the edge of the shore,

a small marble house, with open windows;
music audible, coming from I know not where;
in the house trees with dark leaves, and the
light of a half-shaded lamp ; from one window,
a heavy velvet cloak, with gold fringe, hangs
out with one end falling in the water ; and with
their arms on the cloak, sit *he* and *she*, gazing
into the distance where Venice can be seen.
All this rose as clearly before my mind as
though I had seen it all with my own eyes.
She listened to my nonsense, and said that she
too often dreamed, but that her day-dreams
were of a different sort : she fancied herself in
the deserts of Africa, with some explorer, or
seeking the traces of Franklin in the frozen
Arctic Ocean. She vividly imagined all the
hardships she had to endure, all the difficulties
she had to contend with. . . .

'You have read a lot of travels,' observed her
husband.

'Perhaps,' she responded ; 'but if one must
dream, why need one dream of the unattainable ?'

'And why not ?' I retorted. 'Why is the
poor unattainable to be condemned ? '

'I did not say that,' she said ; 'I meant to
say, what need is there to dream of oneself, of
one's own happiness ? It's useless thinking of
that ; it does not come—why pursue it ? It is
like health ; when you don't think of it, it
means that it's there.'

These words astonished me. There's a great soul in this woman, believe me. . . . From Venice the conversation passed to Italy, to the Italians. Priemkov went away, Vera and I were left alone.

'You have Italian blood in your veins too,' I observed.

'Yes,' she responded; 'shall I show you the portrait of my grandmother?'

'Please do.'

She went to her own sitting-room, and brought out a rather large gold locket. Opening this locket, I saw excellently painted miniature portraits of Madame Eltsov's father and his wife—the peasant woman from Albano. Vera's grandfather struck me by his likeness to his daughter. Only his features, set in a white cloud of powder, seemed even more severe, sharp, and hard, and in his little yellow eyes there was a gleam of a sort of sullen obstinacy. But what a face the Italian woman had, voluptuous, open like a full-blown rose, with prominent, large, liquid eyes, and complacently smiling red lips! Her delicate sensual nostrils seemed dilating and quivering as after recent kisses. The dark cheeks seemed fragrant of glowing heat and health, the luxuriance of youth and womanly power . . . That brow had never done any thinking, and, thank God, she had been depicted in her Albanian dress! The artist (a master) had put a vine in her hair,

which was black as pitch with bright grey high
lights ; this Bacchic ornament was in marvellous
keeping with the expression of her face. And
do you know of whom the face reminded me?
My Manon Lescaut in the black frame. And
what is most wonderful of all, as I looked at
the portrait, I recalled that in Vera too, in spite
of the utter dissimilarity of the features, there
is at times a gleam of something like that
smile, that look. . . .

Yes, I tell you again ; neither she herself nor
any one else in the world knows as yet all that
is latent in her. . . .

By the way—Madame Eltsov, before her
daughter's marriage, told her all her life, her
mother's death, and so on, probably with a view
to her edification. What specially affected
Vera was what she heard about her grandfather,
the mysterious Ladanov. Isn't it owing to
that that she believes in apparitions? It's
strange! She is so pure and bright herself, and
yet is afraid of everything dark and under-
ground, and believes in it. . . .

But enough. Why write all this? However,
as it is written, it may be sent off to you.—
Yours,   P. B.

SEVENTH LETTER

From the SAME to the SAME

M—— VILLAGE, *August* 22, 1850.

I TAKE up my pen ten days after my last letter . . . Oh my dear fellow, I can't hide my feelings any longer! . . . How wretched I am! How I love her! You can imagine with what a thrill of bitterness I write that fatal word. I am not a boy, not a young man even; I am no longer at that stage when to deceive another is almost impossible, but to deceive oneself costs no effort. I know all, and see clearly. I know that I am just on forty, that she's another man's wife, that she loves her husband; I know very well that the unhappy feeling which has gained possession of me can lead to nothing but secret torture and an utter waste of vital energy — I know all that, I expect nothing, and I wish for nothing; but I am not the better off for that. As long as a month ago I began to notice that the attraction she has for me was growing stronger and stronger. This partly troubled me, and partly even delighted me . . . But how could I dream that everything would be repeated with me, which you would have thought could no more come again than youth can? What am I saying! I never loved like this, no, never! Manon Lescauts, Fritilions, these were my idols—such idols can easily be broken; but now . . . only now, I have found out what it is to love a woman. I feel ashamed even to speak of it; but it's so. I'm ashamed . . . Love is egoism any way; and at my years it's not permissible to be an egoist; at thirty-seven one cannot live for oneself; one must live to some purpose, with the aim of doing one's duty, one's work on earth. And I had begun to set to work . . . And here everything is scattered to the winds again, as by a hurricane! Now I understand what I wrote to you in my first letter; I understand now what was the experience I had missed. How suddenly this blow has fallen upon me! I stand and look senselessly forward; a black veil hangs before my eyes; my heart is full of heaviness and dread! I can control myself, I am outwardly calm not only before others, but even in solitude. I can't really rave like a boy! But the worm has crept into my heart, and gnaws it night and day. How will it end? Hitherto I have fretted and suffered when away from her, and in her presence was at peace again at once— now I have no rest even when I am with her, that is what alarms me. Oh my friend, how hard it is to be ashamed of one's tears, to hide them! Only youth may weep; tears are only fitting for the young. . . .

I cannot read over this letter; it has been wrung from me involuntarily, like a groan. I can add nothing, tell you nothing . . . Give me time; I will come to myself, and possess my soul again; I will talk to you like a man, but now I am longing to lay my head on your breast and——

Oh Mephistopheles! you too are no help to me! I stopped short of set purpose, of set purpose I called up what irony is in me, I told myself how ludicrous and mawkish these laments, these outbursts will seem to me in a year, in half a year . . . No, Mephistopheles is powerless, his tooth has lost its edge. . . . Farewell.—Yours, P. B.

EIGHTH LETTER

From the SAME to the SAME

MY DEAR SEMYON NIKOLAITCH,—You have
taken my last letter too much to heart.
You know I have always been given to exaggerating my sensations. It's done as it
were unconsciously in me ; a womanish nature!
In the process of years this will pass away of
course ; but I admit with a sigh I have not
corrected the failing so far. So set your mind
at rest. I am not going to deny the impression made on me by Vera, but I say again, in
all this there is nothing out of the way. For
you to come here, as you write of doing, would
be out of the question, quite. Post over a
thousand versts, God knows with what object
—why, it would be madness! But I am very
grateful for this fresh proof of your affection,
and believe me, I shall never forget it. Your
journey here would be the more out of place as
I mean to come to Petersburg shortly myself.
When I am sitting on your sofa, I shall have a

great deal to tell you, but now I really don't want to; what's the use? I shall only talk nonsense, I dare say, and muddle things up. I will write to you again before I start. And so good-bye for a little while. Be well and happy, and don't worry yourself too much about the fate of—your devoted, **P. B.**

NINTH LETTER

From the SAME to the SAME

P—— VILLAGE, *March* 10, 1853.

I HAVE been a long while without answering
your letter; I have been all these days thinking about it. I felt that it was not idle
curiosity but real friendship that prompted
you, and yet I hesitated whether to follow
your advice, whether to act on your desire.
I have made up my mind at last; I will tell
you everything. Whether my confession will
ease my heart as you suppose, I don't know;
but it seems to me I have no right to hide
from you what has changed my life for ever;
it seems to me, indeed, that I should be
wronging—alas! even more wronging—the
dear being ever in my thoughts, if I did not
confide our mournful secret to the one heart
still dear to me. You alone, perhaps, on earth,
remember Vera, and you judge of her lightly
and falsely; that I cannot endure. You shall
know all. Alas! it can all be told in a couple
of words. All there was between us flashed

by in an instant, like lightning, and like lightning, brought death and ruin. . . . Over two
years have passed since she died ; since I took
up my abode in this remote spot, which I shall
not leave till the end of my days, and everything is still as vivid in my memory, my
wounds are still as fresh, my grief as bitter . . .
I will not complain. Complaints rouse up
sorrow and so ease it, but not mine. I will
begin my story.

Do you remember my last letter—the letter
in which I tried to allay your fears and dis-
suaded you from coming from Petersburg?
You suspected its assumed lightness of tone,
you put no faith in our seeing each other soon;
you were right. On the day before I wrote to
you, I had learnt that I was loved. As I
write these words, I realise how hard it
would be for me to tell my story to the end.
The ever insistent thought of her death will
torture me with redoubled force, I shall be
consumed by these memories. . . . But I will
try to master myself, and will either throw
aside the pen, or will say not a word more
than is necessary. This is how I learnt that
Vera loved me. First of all I must tell you
(and you will believe me) that up to that day
I had absolutely no suspicion. It is true she
had grown pensive at times, which had never
been the way with her before; but I did not
know why this change had come upon her.

At last, one day, the seventh of September —a day memorable for me—this is what happened. You know how I loved her and how wretched I was. I wandered about like an uneasy spirit, and could find no rest. I tried to keep at home, but I could not control myself, and went off to her. I found her alone in her own sitting-room. Priemkov was not at home, he had gone out shooting. When I went in to Vera, she looked intently at me and did not respond to my bow. She was sitting at the window; on her knees lay a book I recognised at once; it was my *Faust*. Her face showed traces of weariness. I sat down opposite her. She asked me to read aloud the scene of Faust with Gretchen, when she asks him if he believes in God. I took the book and began reading. When I had finished, I glanced at her. Her head leaning on the back of her low chair and her arms crossed on her bosom, she was still looking as intently at me.

I don't know why, my heart suddenly began to throb.

'What have you done to me?' she said in a slow voice.

'What?' I articulated in confusion.

'Yes, what have you done to me?' she repeated.

'You mean to say,' I began; 'why did I persuade you to read such books?'

She rose without speaking, and went out of the room. I looked after her.

On the doorway she stopped and turned to me.

'I love you,' she said; 'that's what you have done to me.'

The blood rushed to my head. . . .

'I love you, I am in love with you,' repeated Vera.

She went out and shut the door after her. I will not try to describe what passed within me then. I remember I went out into the garden, made my way into a thicket, leaned against a tree, and how long I stood there, I could not say. I felt faint and numb; a feeling of bliss came over my heart with a rush from time to time. . . . No, I cannot speak of that. Priemkov's voice roused me from my stupor; they had sent to tell him I had come: he had come home from shooting and was looking for me. He was surprised at finding me alone in the garden, without a hat on, and he led me into the house. 'My wife's in the drawing-room,' he observed; 'let's go to her.' You can imagine my sensations as I stepped through the doorway of the drawing-room. Vera was sitting in the corner, at her embroidery frame; I stole a glance at her, and it was a long while before I raised my eyes again. To my amazement, she seemed composed; there was no trace of agitation in what she said, nor in the sound of her voice. At last I brought myself to look at her. Our eyes met . . . She faintly blushed, and bent over her canvas. I began to watch her. She seemed, as it were, perplexed; a cheerless smile hung about her lips now and then.

Priemkov went out. She suddenly raised her head and in a rather loud voice asked me— 'What do you intend to do now?'

I was taken aback, and hurriedly, in a subdued voice, answered, that I intended to do the duty of an honest man—to go away, 'for,' I added, 'I love you, Vera Nikolaevna, you have probably seen that long ago.' She bent over her canvas again and seemed to ponder.

'I must talk with you,' she said; 'come this evening after tea to our little house . . . you know, where you read *Faust*.'

She said this so distinctly that I can't to this day conceive how it was Priemkov, who came into the room at that instant, heard nothing. Slowly, terribly slowly, passed that day. Vera sometimes looked about her with an expression as though she were asking herself if she were not dreaming. And at the same time there was a look of determination in her face; while I . . . I could not recover myself. Vera loves me! These words were continually going round and round in my head; but I did not understand them—I neither understood myself nor her. I could not believe in such unhoped-for, such overwhelming happiness; with an effort I recalled the past, and I too looked and talked as in a dream. . . .

After evening tea, when I had already begun to think how I could steal out of the house unobserved, she suddenly announced of her own accord that she wanted a walk, and asked me to accompany her. I got up, took my hat, and followed her. I did not dare begin to speak, I could scarcely breathe, I awaited her first word, I awaited explanations; but she did not speak. In silence we reached the summer-house, in silence we went into it, and then—I don't know to this day, I can't understand how it happened—we suddenly found ourselves in each other's arms. Some unseen force flung me to her and her to me. In the fading daylight, her face, with the curls tossed back, lighted up for an instant with a smile of self-surrender and tenderness, and our lips met in a kiss. . . .

That kiss was the first and last.

Vera suddenly broke from my arms and with an expression of horror in her wide open eyes staggered back——

'Look round,' she said in a shaking voice; 'do you see nothing?'

I turned round quickly.

'Nothing. Why, do you see something?'

'Not now, but I did.'

She drew deep, gasping breaths.

'Whom? what?'

'My mother,' she said slowly, and she began trembling all over. I shivered too, as though with cold. I suddenly felt ashamed, as though I were guilty. And indeed, wasn't I guilty at that instant?

'Nonsense!' I began; 'what do you mean? Tell me rather——'

'No, for God's sake, no!' she interposed, clutching her head. 'This is madness— I'm going out of my mind. . . . One can't play with this—it's death. . . . Good-bye. . . .'

I held out my hands to her.

'Stay, for God's sake, for an instant,' I cried in an involuntary outburst. I didn't know what I was saying and could scarcely stand upright. 'For God's sake . . . it is too cruel!'

She glanced at me.

'To-morrow, to-morrow evening,' she said, 'not to-day, I beseech you — go away to-day . . . to-morrow evening come to the garden gate, near the lake. I will be there, I will come. . . . I swear to you I will come,' she added with passion, and her eyes shone; 'whoever may hinder me, I swear! I will tell you everything, only let me go to-day.'

And before I could utter a word she was gone. Utterly distraught, I stayed where I was. My head was in a whirl. Across the mad rapture, which filled my whole being, there began to steal a feeling of apprehension.

. . . I looked round. The dim, damp room in which I was standing oppressed me with its low roof and dark walls.

I went out and walked with dejected steps towards the house. Vera was waiting for me on the terrace; she went into the house directly I drew near, and at once retreated to her bedroom.

I went away.

How I spent the night and the next day till the evening I can't tell you. I only remember that I lay, my face hid in my hands, I recalled her smile before our kiss, I whispered—'At last, she . . .'

I recalled, too, Madame Eltsov's words, which Vera had repeated to me. She had said to her once, 'You are like ice; until you melt as strong as stone, but directly you melt there's nothing of you left.'

Another thing recurred to my mind; Vera and I had once been talking of talent, ability.

'There's only one thing I can do,' she said; 'keep silent till the last minute.'

I did not understand it in the least at the time.

'But what is the meaning of her fright?' I wondered — 'Can she really have seen Madame Eltsov? Imagination!' I thought, and again I gave myself up to the emotions of expectation.

It was on that day I wrote you,—with what

thoughts in my head it hurts me to recall—that deceitful letter.

In the evening—the sun had not yet set—I took up my stand about fifty paces from the garden gate in a tall thicket on the edge of the lake. I had come from home on foot. I will confess to my shame; fear, fear of the most cowardly kind, filled my heart; I was incessantly starting . . . but I had no feeling of remorse. Hiding among the twigs, I kept continual watch on the little gate. It did not open. The sun set, the evening drew on ; then the stars came out, and the sky turned black. No one appeared. I was in a fever. Night came on. I could bear it no longer; I came cautiously out of the thicket and stole down to the gate. Everything was still in the garden. I called Vera, in a whisper, called a second time, a third. . . . No voice called back. Half-an-hour more passed by, and an hour; it became quite dark. I was worn out by suspense; I drew the gate towards me, opened it at once, and on tip-toe, like a thief, walked towards the house. I stopped in the shadow of a lime-tree.

Almost all the windows in the house had lights in them ; people were moving to and fro in the house. This surprised me ; my watch, as far as I could make out in the dim starlight, said half-past eleven. Suddenly I heard a noise near the house ; a carriage drove out of the courtyard.

'Visitors, it seems,' I thought. Losing every hope of seeing Vera, I made my way out of the garden and walked with rapid steps homewards. It was a dark September night, but warm and windless. The feeling, not so much of annoyance as of sadness, which had taken possession of me, gradually disappeared, and I got home, rather tired from my rapid walk, but soothed by the peacefulness of the night, happy and almost light-hearted. I went to my room, dismissed Timofay, and without undressing, flung myself on my bed and plunged into reverie.

At first my day-dreams were sweet, but soon I noticed a curious change in myself. I began to feel a sort of secret gnawing anxiety, a sort of deep, inward uneasiness. I could not understand what it arose from, but I began to feel sick and sad, as though I were menaced by some approaching trouble, as though some one dear to me were suffering at that instant and calling on me for help. A wax candle on the table burnt with a small, steady flame, the pendulum swung with a heavy, regular tick. I leant my head on my hand and fell to gazing into the empty half-dark of my lonely room. I thought of Vera, and my heart failed me; all, at which I had so rejoiced, struck me, as it ought to have done, as unhappiness, as hopeless ruin. The feeling of apprehension grew and grew; I could not lie still any longer; I suddenly fancied again that some one was calling me in a voice of entreaty. . . . I raised my head and shuddered; I had not been mistaken; a pitiful cry floated out of the distance and rang faintly resounding on the dark window-panes. I was frightened; I jumped off the bed; I opened the window. A distinct moan broke into the room and, as it were, hovered about me. Chilled with terror, I drank in its last dying echoes. It seemed as though some one were being killed in the distance and the luckless wretch were beseeching in vain for mercy. Whether it was an owl hooting in the wood or some other creature that uttered this wail, I did not think to consider at the time, but, like Mazeppa, I called back in answer to the ill-omened sound.

'Vera, Vera!' I cried; 'is it you calling me?' Timofay, sleepy and amazed, appeared before me.

I came to my senses, drank a glass of water, and went into another room; but sleep did not come to me. My heart throbbed painfully though not rapidly. I could not abandon myself to dreams of happiness again; I dared not believe in it.

Next day, before dinner, I went to the Priemkovs'. Priemkov met me with a careworn face.

'My wife is ill,' he began; 'she is in bed; I sent for a doctor.'

'What is the matter with her?'

'I can't make out. Yesterday evening she went into the garden and suddenly came back quite beside herself, panic-stricken. Her maid ran for me. I went in, and asked my wife what was wrong. She made no answer, and so she has lain; by night delirium set in. In her delirium she said all sorts of things; she mentioned you. The maid told me an extraordinary thing; that Vera's mother appeared to her in the garden; she fancied she was coming to meet her with open arms.'

You can imagine what I felt at these words.

'Of course that's nonsense,' Priemkov went on; 'though I must admit that extraordinary things have happened to my wife in that way.'

'And you say Vera Nikolaevna is very unwell?'

'Yes: she was very bad in the night; now she is wandering.'

'What did the doctor say?'

'The doctor said that the disease was undefined as yet. . . .'

March 12.

I cannot go on as I began, dear friend; it costs me too much effort and re-opens my wounds too cruelly. The disease, to use the doctor's words, became defined, and Vera died of it. She did not live a fortnight after the fatal day of our momentary interview. I saw

her once more before her death. I have no
memory more heart-rending. I had already
learned from the doctor that there was no
hope. Late in the evening, when every one in
the house was in bed, I stole to the door of
her room and looked in at her. Vera lay in
her bed, with closed eyes, thin and small, with
a feverish flush on her cheeks. I gazed at her
as though turned to stone. All at once she
opened her eyes, fastened them upon me,
scrutinised me, and stretching out a wasted
hand—

> 'Was will er an dem heiligen Ort
> Der da . . . der dort . . .'[1]

she articulated, in a voice so terrible that I
rushed headlong away. Almost all through
her illness, she raved about *Faust* and her
mother, whom she sometimes called Martha,
sometimes Gretchen's mother.

Vera died. I was at her burying. Ever
since then I have given up everything and am
settled here for ever.

Think now of what I have told you; think
of her, of that being so quickly brought to
destruction. How it came to pass, how explain this incomprehensible intervention of the
dead in the affairs of the living, I don't know
and never shall know. But you must admit
that it is not a fit of whimsical spleen, as you

---

[1] *Faust*, Part I., Last Scene.

express it, which has driven me to retire from the world. I am not what I was, as you knew me; I believe in a great deal now which I did not believe formerly. All this time I have thought so much of that unhappy woman (I had almost said, girl), of her origin, of the secret play of fate, which we in our blindness call blind chance. Who knows what seeds each man living on earth leaves behind him, which are only destined to come up after his death? Who can say by what mysterious bond a man's fate is bound up with his children's, his descendants'; how his yearnings are reflected in them, and how they are punished for his errors? We must all submit and bow our heads before the Unknown.

Yes, Vera perished, while I was untouched. I remember, when I was a child, we had in my home a lovely vase of transparent alabaster. Not a spot sullied its virgin whiteness. One day when I was left alone, I began shaking the stand on which it stood . . . the vase suddenly fell down and broke to shivers. I was numb with horror, and stood motionless before the fragments. My father came in, saw me, and said, 'There, see what you have done; we shall never have our lovely vase again; now there is no mending it!' I sobbed. I felt I had committed a crime.

I grew into a man—and thoughtlessly broke a vessel a thousand times more precious. . . .

In vain I tell myself that I could not have dreamed of such a sudden catastrophe, that it struck me too with its suddenness, that I did not even suspect what sort of nature Vera was. She certainly knew how to be silent till the last minute. I ought to have run away directly I felt that I loved her, that I loved a married woman. But I stayed, and that fair being was shattered, and with despair I gaze at the work of my own hands.

Yes, Madame Eltsov took jealous care of her daughter. She guarded her to the end, and at the first incautious step bore her away with her to the grave!

It is time to make an end. . . . I have not told one hundredth part of what I ought to have; but this has been enough for me. Let all that has flamed up fall back again into the depths of my heart. . . . In conclusion, I say to you—one conviction I have gained from the experience of the last years—life is not jest and not amusement; life is not even enjoyment . . . life is hard labour. Renunciation, continual renunciation — that is its secret meaning, its solution. Not the fulfilment of cherished dreams and aspirations, however lofty they may be—the fulfilment of duty, that is what must be the care of man. Without laying on himself chains, the iron chains of duty, he cannot reach without a fall the end of his career. But in youth we think—the freer

the better, the further one will get. Youth
may be excused for thinking so. But it is
shameful to delude oneself when the stern
face of truth has looked one in the eyes at
last.

Good-bye! In old days I would have added,
be happy; now I say to you, try to live, it is
not so easy as it seems. Think of me, not in
hours of sorrow, but in hours of contemplation,
and keep in your heart the image of Vera in
all its pure stainlessness. . . . Once more,
good-bye!—Yours,   P. B.

1855.

ACIA

ACIA

I

AT that time I was five-and-twenty, began
N. N.,—it was in days long past, as you perceive. I had only just gained my freedom and
gone abroad, not to 'finish my education,' as
the phrase was in those days ; I simply wanted
to have a look at God's world. I was young,
and in good health and spirits, and had plenty
of money. Troubles had not yet had time to
gather about me. I existed without thought,
did as I liked, lived like the lilies of the field,
in fact. It never occurred to me in those days
that man is not a plant, and cannot go on living
like one for long. Youth will eat gilt gingerbread and fancy it's daily bread too ; but the
time comes when you're in want of dry bread
even. There's no need to go into that, though.

I travelled without any sort of aim, without
a plan ; I stopped wherever I liked the place,
and went on again directly I felt a desire to
see new faces—faces, nothing else. I was interested in people exclusively ; I hated famous

monuments and museums of curiosities, the very sight of a guide produced in me a sense of weariness and anger; I was almost driven crazy in the Dresden 'Grüne-Gewölbe.' Nature affected me extremely, but I did not care for the so-called beauties of nature, extraordinary mountains, precipices, and waterfalls; I did not like nature to obtrude, to force itself upon me. But faces, living human faces—people's talk, and gesture, and laughter—that was what was absolutely necessary to me. In a crowd I always had a special feeling of ease and comfort. I enjoyed going where others went, shouting when others shouted, and at the same time I liked to look at the others shouting. It amused me to watch people ... though I didn't even watch them—I simply stared at them with a sort of delighted, ever-eager curiosity. But I am diverging again.

And so twenty years ago I was staying in the little German town Z., on the left bank of the Rhine. I was seeking solitude; I had just been stabbed to the heart by a young widow, with whom I had made acquaintance at a watering-place. She was very pretty and clever, and flirted with every one—with me, too, poor sinner. At first she had positively encouraged me, but later on she cruelly wounded my feelings, sacrificing me for a red-faced Bavarian lieutenant. It must be owned, the wound to my heart was not a very deep one;

but I thought it my duty to give myself up
for a time to gloom and solitude—youth will
find amusement in anything!—and so I settled
at Z.

I liked the little town for its situation on the
slope of two high hills, its ruined walls and
towers, its ancient lime-trees, its steep bridge
over the little clear stream that falls into the
Rhine, and, most of all, for its excellent wine.
In the evening, directly after sunset (it was
June), very pretty flaxen-haired German girls
used to walk about its narrow streets and
articulate 'Guten Abend' in agreeable voices
on meeting a stranger,—some of them did not
go home even when the moon had risen behind
the pointed roofs of the old houses, and the
tiny stones that paved the street could be distinctly seen in its still beams. I liked wandering about the town at that time; the moon
seemed to keep a steady watch on it from the
clear sky; and the town was aware of this
steady gaze, and stood quiet and attentive,
bathed in the moonlight, that peaceful light
which is yet softly exciting to the soul. The
cock on the tall Gothic bell-tower gleamed a
pale gold, the same gold sheen glimmered in
waves over the black surface of the stream;
slender candles (the German is a thrifty soul!)
twinkled modestly in the narrow windows under
the slate roofs; branches of vine thrust out their
twining tendrils mysteriously from behind stone

walls; something flitted into the shade by the old-fashioned well in the three-cornered market place; the drowsy whistle of the night watchman broke suddenly on the silence, a good-natured dog gave a subdued growl, while the air simply caressed the face, and the lime-trees smelt so sweet that unconsciously the lungs drew in deeper and deeper breaths of it, and the name 'Gretchen' hung, half exclamation, half question, on the lips.

The little town of Z. lies a mile and a half from the Rhine. I used often to walk to look at the majestic river, and would spend long hours on a stone-seat under a huge solitary ash-tree, musing, not without some mental effort, on the faithless widow. A little statue of a Madonna, with an almost childish face and a red heart, pierced with swords, on her bosom, peeped mournfully out of the branches of the ash-tree. On the opposite bank of the river was the little town L., somewhat larger than that in which I had taken up my quarters. One evening I was sitting on my favourite seat, gazing at the sky, the river, and the vineyards. In front of me flaxen-headed boys were scrambling up the sides of a boat that had been pulled ashore, and turned with its tarred bottom upwards. Sailing-boats moved slowly by with slightly dimpling sails; the greenish waters glided by, swelling and faintly rumbling. All of a sudden sounds of music drifted across to me ; I listened. A waltz was being played in the town of L. The double bass boomed spasmodically, the sound of the fiddle floated across indistinctly now and then, the flute was tootling briskly.

'What's that?' I inquired of an old man who came up to me, in a plush waistcoat, blue stockings, and shoes with buckles.

'That,' he replied, after first shifting his pipe from one corner of his mouth to the other, 'is the students come over from B. to a com-mersh.'

'I 'll have a look at this commersh,' I thought. 'I 've never been over to L. either.' I sought out a ferryman, and went over to the other side.

II

EVERY one, perhaps, may not know what such a commersh is. It is a solemn festival of a special sort, at which students meet together who are of one district or brotherhood (Landsmannschaft). Almost all who take part in the commersh wear the time-honoured costume of German students: Hungarian jackets, big boots, and little caps, with bands round them of certain colours. The students generally assemble to a dinner, presided over by their senior member, and they keep up the festivities till morning—drinking, singing songs, 'Landesvater,' 'Gaudeamus,' etc., smoking, and reviling the Philistines. Sometimes they hire an orchestra.

Just such a commersh was going on in L., in front of a little inn, with the sign of the Sun, in the garden looking on to the street. Flags were flying over the inn and over the garden; the students were sitting at tables under the pollard lime-trees; a huge bull-dog was lying under one of the tables; on one side, in an ivy-covered arbour, were the musicians, playing away zealously, and continually invigorating themselves with beer. A good many people had collected in the street, before the low garden wall; the worthy citizens of L. could not let slip a chance of staring at visitors. I too mingled in the crowd of spectators. I enjoyed watching the students' faces; their embraces, exclamations, the innocent affectations of youth, the fiery glances, the laughter without cause—the sweetest laughter in the world—all this joyous effervescence of young, fresh life, this eager pushing forward—anywhere, so long as it's forward—the simple-hearted freedom moved me and stirred me.

'Couldn't I join them?' I was wondering. . . .

'Acia, have you had enough of it?' I heard a man's voice say suddenly, in Russian, just behind me.

'Let's stay a little longer,' answered another voice, a woman's, in the same language.

I turned quickly round. . . . My eyes fell on a handsome young man in a peaked cap and a loose short jacket. He had on his arm a young girl, not very tall, wearing a straw hat, which concealed all the upper part of her face.

'You are Russians,' fell involuntarily from my lips.

The young man smiled and answered—

'Yes, we are Russians.'

'I never expected . . . in such an out of the way place,' I was beginning—

'Nor did we,' he interrupted me. 'Well, so much the better. Let me introduce myself. My name's Gagin, and this is my——' he hesitated for an instant, 'my sister. What is your name, may I ask?'

I told him my name, and we got into conversation. I found out that Gagin was travelling, like me, for his amusement; that he had arrived a week before at L., and was staying on there. To tell the truth, I was not eager to make friends with Russians abroad. I used to recognise them a long way off by their walk, the cut of their clothes, and, most of all, by the expression of their faces which was self-complacent and supercilious, often imperious, but would all of a sudden change, and give place to an expression of shyness and cautiousness. . . . The whole man would suddenly be on his guard, his eyes would shift uneasily. . . . 'Mercy upon us! Haven't I said something silly; aren't they laughing at me?' those restless eyes seem to ask. . . . An instant later and haughtiness has regained its sway over the physiognomy, varied at times by a look of dull blankness. Yes, I avoided Russians; but I liked Gagin at once. There are faces in the world of that happy sort; every one is glad to look at them, as though they warmed or soothed one in some way. Gagin had just such a face—sweet and kind, with large soft eyes and soft curly hair. He spoke in such a way that even if you did not see his face, you could tell by the mere sound of his voice that he was smiling!

The girl, whom he had called his sister, struck me at the first glance as very charming. There was something individual, characteristic in the lines of her dark, round face, with its small, fine nose, almost childish cheeks, and clear black eyes. She was gracefully built, but hardly seemed to have reached her full development yet. She was not in the least like her brother.

'Will you come home with us?' Gagin said to me; 'I think we've stared enough at the Germans. Our fellows, to be sure, would have broken the windows, and smashed up the chairs, but these chaps are very sedate. What do you say, Acia, shall we go home?'

The girl nodded her head in assent.

'We live outside the town,' Gagin continued, 'in a vineyard, in a lonely little house, high up. It's delightful there, you'll see. Our landlady promised to make us some junket. It will soon be dark now, and you had much better cross the Rhine by moonlight.'

We set off. Through the low gates of the town (it was enclosed on all sides by an ancient wall of cobble-stones, even the barbicans had not all fallen into ruins at that time), we came out into the open country, and after walking a hundred paces beside a stone wall, we came to a standstill before a little narrow gate. Gagin opened it, and led us along a steep path up the mountain-side. On the slopes on both sides was the vineyard; the sun had just set, and a delicate rosy flush lay on the green vines, on the tall poles, on the dry earth, which was dotted with big and little stones, and on the white wall of the little cottage, with sloping black beams, and four bright little windows, which stood at the very top of the mountain we had climbed up.

'Here is our house!' cried Gagin, directly we began to approach the cottage, 'and here's the landlady bringing in the junket. Guten Abend, Madame! . . . We'll come in to supper directly; but first,' he added, 'look round . . . isn't it a view?'

The view certainly was marvellous. The Rhine lay at our feet, all silvery between its green banks; in one place it glowed with the purple and gold of the sunset. The little town, nestling close to the river-bank, displayed all its streets and houses; sloping hills and meadows ran in wide stretches in all directions. Below it was fine, but above was finer still; I was specially impressed by the depth and purity of the sky, the radiant transparency of the atmosphere. The fresh, light air seemed softly quivering and undulating, as though it too were more free and at ease on the heights.

'You have chosen delightful lodgings,' I observed.

'It was Acia found it,' answered Gagin; 'come, Acia,' he went on, 'see after the supper. Let everything be brought out here. We will have supper in the open air. We can hear the music better here. Have you ever noticed,' he added, turning to me, 'a waltz is often poor stuff close by—vulgar, coarse music—but in the distance, it's exquisite! it fairly stirs every romantic chord within one.'

Acia (her real name was Anna, but Gagin called her Acia, and you must let me do the same), went into the house, and soon came back with the landlady. They were carrying together a big tray, with a bowl of junket, plates, spoons, sugar, fruit, and bread. We sat down and began supper. Acia took off her hat; her black hair cropped short and combed, like a boy's, fell in thick curls on her neck and ears. At first she was shy of me; but Gagin said to her—

'Come, Acia, come out of your shell! he won't bite.'

She smiled, and a little while after she began talking to me of her own accord. I had never seen such a restless creature. She did not sit still for a single instant; she got up, ran off into the house, and ran back again, hummed in an undertone, often laughed, and in a very strange way; she seemed to laugh, not at what she heard, but at the different ideas that crossed her mind. Her big eyes looked out boldly, brightly, directly, but sometimes her eyelids faintly drooped, and then their expression instantaneously became deep and tender.

We chatted away for a couple of hours. The daylight had long died away, and the evening glow, at first fiery, then clear and red, then pale and dim, had slowly melted away and passed into night, but our conversation still went on, as quiet and peaceful as the air around us. Gagin ordered a bottle of Rhine wine; we drank it between us, slowly and deliberately. The music floated across to us as before, its strains seemed sweeter and tenderer; lights were burning in the town and on the river. Acia suddenly let her head fall, so that her curls dropped into her eyes, ceased speaking, and sighed. Then she said she was sleepy, and went indoors. I saw, though, that she stood a long while at the unopened window without lighting a candle. At last the moon rose and began shining upon the Rhine; everything turned to light and darkness, everything was transformed, even the wine in our cut-glass tumblers gleamed with a mysterious light. The wind drooped, as it were, folded its wings and sank to rest; the fragrant warmth of night rose in whiffs from the earth.

'It's time I was going!' I cried, 'or else perhaps, there'll be no getting a ferryman.'

'Yes, it's time to start,' Gagin assented.

We went down the path. Suddenly we heard the rolling of the stones behind us; it was Acia coming after us.

'Aren't you asleep?' asked her brother; but, without answering a word, she ran by us. The last, smouldering lamps, lighted by the students in the garden of the inn, threw a light on the leaves of the trees from below, giving them a fantastic and festive look. We found Acia at the river's edge; she was talking to a ferryman. I jumped into the boat, and said good-bye to my new friends. Gagin promised to pay me a visit next day; I pressed his hand, and held out my hand to Acia; but she only looked at me and shook her head. The boat pushed off and floated on the rapid river. The ferryman, a sturdy old man, buried his oars in the dark water, and pulled with great effort.

'You are in the streak of moonlight, you have broken it up,' Acia shouted to me.

I dropped my eyes; the waters eddied round the boat, blacker than ever.

'Good-bye!' I heard her voice.

'Till to-morrow,' Gagin said after her.

The boat reached the other side. I got out and looked about me. No one could be seen now on the opposite bank. The streak of moonlight stretched once more like a bridge of gold right across the river. Like a farewell, the air of the old-fashioned Lanner waltz drifted across. Gagin was right ; I felt every chord in my heart vibrating in response to its seductive melody. I started homewards across the darkening fields, drinking in slowly the fragrant air, and reached my room, deeply stirred by the voluptuous languor of vague, endless anticipation. I felt happy. . . . But why was I happy ? I desired nothing, I thought of nothing. . . . I was happy.

Almost laughing from excess of sweet, light-hearted emotions, I dived into my bed, and was just closing my eyes, when all at once it struck me that I had not once all the evening remembered my cruel charmer. . . . 'What's the meaning of it?' I wondered to myself; 'is it possible I'm not in love?' But though I asked myself this question, I fell asleep, I think, at once, like a baby in its cradle.

III

NEXT morning (I was awake, but had not yet begun to get up), I heard the tap of a stick on my window, and a voice I knew at once for Gagin's hummed—

> 'Art thou asleep? with the guitar
> Will I awaken thee . . .'

I made haste to open the door to him.

'Good-morning,' said Gagin, coming in; 'I'm disturbing you rather early, but only see what a morning it is. Fresh, dewy, larks singing . . .'

With his curly, shining hair, his open neck and rosy cheeks, he was fresh as the morning himself.

I dressed; we went out into the garden, sat down on a bench, ordered coffee, and proceeded to talk. Gagin told me his plans for the future; he possessed a moderate fortune, was not dependent on any one, and wanted to devote himself to painting. He only regretted that he had not had more sense sooner, but had wasted so much time doing nothing. I too referred to my projects, and incidentally confided to him the secret of my unhappy love. He listened to me amiably, but, so far as I could observe, I did not arouse in him any very strong sympathy with my passion. Sighing once or twice after me, for civility's sake, Gagin suggested that I should go home with him and look at his sketches. I agreed at once.

We did not find Acia. She had, the landlady told us, gone to the 'ruin.' A mile and a half from L. were the remains of a feudal castle. Gagin showed me all his canvases. In his sketches there was a good deal of life and truth, a certain breadth and freedom; but not one of them was finished, and the drawing struck me as careless and incorrect. I gave candid expression to my opinion.

'Yes, yes,' he assented, with a sigh; 'you're right; it's all very poor and crude; what's to be done? I haven't had the training I ought to have had; besides, one's cursed Slavonic slackness gets the better of one. While one dreams of work, one soars away in eagle flight; one fancies one's going to shake the earth out of its place—but when it comes to doing anything, one's weak and weary directly.'

I began trying to cheer him up, but he waved me off, and bundling his sketches up together, threw them on the sofa.

'If I've patience, something may be made of me,' he muttered; 'if I haven't, I shall remain a half-baked noble amateur. Come we'd better be looking for Acia.'

We went out.

IV

THE road to the ruin went twisting down
the steep incline into a narrow wooded valley;
at the bottom ran a stream, noisily threading
its way through the pebbles, as though in haste
to flow into the great river, peacefully shining
beyond the dark ridge of the deep indented
mountain crest. Gagin called my attention to
some places where the light fell specially finely;
one could see in his words that, even if not a
painter, he was undoubtedly an artist. The
ruin soon came into sight. On the very summit
of the naked rock rose a square tower, black all
over, still strong, but, as it were, cleft in two by
a longitudinal crack. Mossy walls adjoined
the tower; here and there ivy clung about it;
wind-twisted bushes hung down from the grey
battlements and crumbling arches. A stray
path led up to the gates, still standing entire.
We had just reached them, when suddenly a
girl's figure darted up in front of us, ran swiftly
over a heap of debris, and stood on the projecting part of the wall, right over the precipice.

'Why, it's Acia!' cried Gagin; 'the mad

ACIA

thing.' We went through the gates and found
ourselves in a small courtyard, half overgrown
with crab-apple trees and nettles. On the projecting ledge, Acia actually was sitting. She
turned and faced us, laughing, but did not move.
Gagin shook his finger at her, while I loudly
reproached her for her recklessness.

'That's enough,' Gagin said to me in a whisper; 'don't tease her; you don't know what she
is; she'd very likely climb right up on to the
tower. Look, you'd better be admiring the
intelligence of the people of these parts!'

I looked round. In a corner, ensconced in
a tiny, wooden hut, an old woman was knit-
ting a stocking, and looking at us through her
spectacles. She sold beer, gingerbread, and
seltzer water to tourists. We seated ourselves
on a bench, and began drinking some fairly cold
beer out of heavy pewter pots. Acia still sat
without moving, with her feet tucked under her,
and a muslin scarf wrapped round her head;
her graceful figure stood out distinctly and
finely against the clear sky; but I looked at
her with a feeling of hostility. The evening
before I had detected something forced, something not quite natural about her. . . . 'She's
trying to impress us,' I thought; 'whatever for?
What a childish trick.' As though guessing
my thoughts, she suddenly turned a rapid,
searching glance upon me, laughed again,
leaped in two bounds from the wall, and going

up to the old woman, asked her for a glass of water.

'Do you think I am thirsty?' she said, addressing her brother; 'no; there are some flowers on the walls, which must be watered.'

Gagin made her no reply; and with the glass in her hand, she began scrambling over the ruins, now and then stopping, bending down, and with comic solemnity pouring a few drops of water, which sparkled brightly in the sun. Her movements were very charming, but I felt, as before, angry with her, even while I could not help admiring her lightness and agility. At one dangerous place she purposely screamed, and then laughed. . . . I felt still more annoyed with her.

'Why, she climbs like a goat,' the old woman mumbled, turning for an instant from her stocking.

At last, Acia had emptied the glass, and with a saucy swing she walked back to us. A queer smile was faintly twitching at her eyebrows, nostrils, and lips; her dark eyes were screwed up with a half insolent, half merry look.

'You consider my behaviour improper,' her face seemed to say; 'all the same, I know you're admiring me.'

'Well done, Acia, well done,' Gagin said in a low voice.

She seemed all at once overcome with shame,

he dropped her long eyelashes, and sat down beside us with a guilty air. At that moment I got for the first time a good look at her face, the most changeable face I had ever seen. A few instants later it had turned quite pale, and wore an intense, almost mournful expression, its very features seemed larger, sterner, simpler. She completely subsided. We walked round the ruins (Acia followed us), and admired the views. Meanwhile it was getting near dinner-time. As he paid the old woman, Gagin asked for another mug of beer, and turning to me, cried with a sly face—

'To the health of the lady of your heart.'

'Why, has he—have you such a lady?' Acia asked suddenly.

'Why, who hasn't?' retorted Gagin.

Acia seemed pensive for an instant; then her face changed, the challenging, almost insolent smile came back once more.

On the way home she kept laughing, and was more mischievous again. She broke off a long branch, put it on her shoulder, like a gun, and tied her scarf round her head. I remember we met a numerous family of light-haired affected English people; they all, as though at a word of command, looked Acia up and down with their glassy eyes in chilly amazement, while she started singing aloud, as though in defiance of them. When she reached home, she went straight to her own room, and only appeared when dinner was on the table. She was dressed in her best clothes, had carefully arranged her hair, laced herself in at the waist, and put on gloves. At dinner she behaved very decorously, almost affectedly, hardly tasting anything, and drinking water out of a wineglass. She obviously wanted to show herself in a new character before me—the character of a well-bred, refined young lady. Gagin did not check her; one could see that it was his habit to humour her in everything. He merely glanced at me good-humouredly now and then, and slightly shrugged his shoulders, as though he would say—'She's a baby; don't be hard on her.' Directly dinner was over, Acia got up, made us a curtsey, and putting on her hat, asked Gagin if she might go to see Frau Luise.

'Since when do you ask leave,' he answered with his invariable smile, a rather embarrassed smile this time; 'are you bored with us?'

'No; but I promised Frau Luise yesterday to go and see her; besides, I thought you would like better being alone. Mr. N. (she indicated me) will tell you something more about himself.'

She went out.

'Frau Luise,' Gagin began, trying to avoid meeting my eyes, 'is the widow of a former burgomaster here, a good-natured, but silly old woman. She has taken a great fancy to Acia. Acia has a passion for making friends with people of a lower class; I've noticed, it's always pride that's at the root of that. She's pretty well spoilt with me, as you see,' he went on after a brief pause: 'but what would you have me do? I can't be exacting with any one, and with her less than any one else. I am *bound* not to be hard on her.'

I was silent. Gagin changed the conversation. The more I saw of him, the more strongly was I attracted by him. I soon understood him. His was a typically Russian nature, truthful, honest, simple; but, unhappily, without energy, lacking tenacity and inward fire. Youth was not boiling over within him, but shone with a subdued light. He was very sweet and clever, but I could not picture to myself what he would become in ripe manhood. An artist . . . without intense, incessant toil, there is no being an artist . . . and as for toil, I mused, watching his soft features, listening to his slow deliberate talk, 'no, you'll never toil, you don't know how to put pressure on yourself.' But not to love him was an impossibility; one's heart was simply drawn to him. We spent four hours together, sometimes sitting on the sofa, sometimes walking slowly up and down before the house; and in those four hours we became intimate friends.

The sun was setting, and it was time for me to go home. Acia had not yet come back.

'What a reckless thing she is,' said Gagin.

' Shall I come along with you ? We'll turn in at Frau Luise's on the way. I'll ask whether she's there. It's not far out of the way.'

We went down into the town, and turning off into a narrow, crooked little by-street, stopped before a house four storeys high, and with two windows abreast in each storey. The second storey projected beyond the first, the third and fourth stood out still further than the second ; the whole house, with its crumbling carving, its two stout columns below, its pointed brick roof, and the projecting piece on the attic poking out like a beak, looked like a huge, crouching bird.

' Acia,' shouted Gagin, ' are you here ? '

A window, with a light in it in the third storey, rattled and opened, and we saw Acia's dark head. Behind her peered out the toothless and dim-sighted face of an old German woman.

' I'm here,' said Acia, leaning roguishly out with her elbows on the window-sill ; ' I'm quite contented here. Hullo there, catch,' she added, flinging Gagin a twig of geranium ; 'imagine I'm the lady of your heart.'

Frau Luise laughed.

' N. is going,' said Gagin ; ' he wants to say good-bye to you.'

' Really,' said Acia ; ' in that case give him my geranium, and I'll come back directly.'

She slammed-to the window and seemed to

be kissing Frau Luise.   Gagin offered me the twig without a word.   I put it in my pocket in silence, went on to the ferry, and crossed over to the other side of the river.

I remember I went home thinking of nothing in particular, but with a strange load at my heart, when I was suddenly struck by a strong familiar scent, rare in Germany.   I stood still, and saw near the road a small bed of hemp. Its fragrance of the steppes instantaneously brought my own country to my mind, and stirred a passionate longing for it in my heart.   I longed to breathe Russian air, to tread on Russian soil.   'What am I doing here, why am I trailing about in foreign countries among strangers?'   I cried, and the dead weight I had felt at my heart suddenly passed into a bitter, stinging emotion.   I reached home in quite a different frame of mind from the evening before.   I felt almost enraged, and it was a long while before I could recover my equanimity.   I was beset by a feeling of anger I could not explain.   At last I sat down, and bethinking myself of my faithless widow (I wound up every day regularly by dreaming, as in duty bound, of this lady), I pulled out one of her letters.   But I did not even open it; my thoughts promptly took another turn.   I began dreaming—dreaming of Acia.   I recollected that Gagin had, in the course of conversation, hinted at certain difficulties, obstacles in the way of his returning 'to Russia. . . . 'Come, is she his sister ?' I said aloud.

I undressed, got into bed, and tried to get to sleep ; but an hour later I was sitting up again in bed, propped up with my elbow on the pillow, and was once more thinking about this 'whimsical chit of a girl with the affected laugh.' . . . 'She's the figure of the little Galatea of Raphael in the Farnesino,' I murmured : 'yes ; and she's not his sister——'

The widow's letter lay tranquil and undisturbed on the floor, a white patch in the moonlight.

V

NEXT morning I went again to L——. I persuaded myself I wanted to see Gagin, but secretly I was tempted to go and see what Acia would do, whether she would be as whimsical as on the previous day. I found them both in their sitting-room, and strange to say—possibly because I had been thinking so much that night and morning of Russia— Acia struck me as a typically Russian girl, and a girl of the humbler class, almost like a Russian servant-girl. She wore an old gown, she had combed her hair back behind her ears, and was sitting still as a mouse at the window, working at some embroidery in a frame, quietly, demurely, as though she had never done anything else all her life. She said scarcely anything, looked quietly at her work, and her features wore such an ordinary, commonplace expression, that I could not help thinking of our Katias and Mashas at home in Russia. To complete the resemblance she started singing in a low voice, 'Little mother, little dove.' I looked at her little face, which was rather yellow and listless, I thought of my dreams of the previous night, and I felt a pang of regret for something.

It was exquisite weather. Gagin announced that he was going to make a sketch to-day from nature; I asked him if he would let me go with him, whether I shouldn't be in his way.

'On the contrary,' he assured me; 'you may give me some good advice.'

He put on a hat à la Vandyck, and a blouse, took a canvas under his arm, and set out; I sauntered after him. Acia stayed at home. Gagin, as he went out, asked her to see that the soup wasn't too thin; Acia promised to look into the kitchen. Gagin went as far as the valley I knew already, sat down on a stone, and began to sketch a hollow oak with spreading branches. I lay on the grass and took out a book; but I didn't read two pages, and he simply spoiled a sheet of paper; we did little else but talk, and as far as I am competent to judge, we talked rather cleverly and subtly of the right method of working, of what we must avoid, and what one must cling to, and wherein lay the significance of the artist in our age. Gagin, at last, decided that he was not in the mood to-day, and lay down beside me on the grass. And then our youthful eloquence flowed freely; fervent, pensive, enthusiastic by turns, but consisting almost always of those vague generalities into which a Russian is so ready to expand. When we had talked to our hearts' content, and were full of a feeling of satisfaction as though we had got something done, achieved some sort of success, we returned home. I found Acia just as I had left her; however assiduously I watched her I could not detect a shade of coquetry, nor a sign of an intentionally assumed rôle in her; this time it was impossible to reproach her for artificiality.

'Aha!' said Gagin; 'she has imposed fasting and penance on herself.'

Towards evening she yawned several times with obvious genuineness, and went early to her room. I myself soon said good-bye to Gagin, and as I went home, I had no dreams of any kind; that day was spent in sober sensations. I remember, however, as I lay down to sleep, I involuntarily exclaimed aloud—

'What a chameleon the girl is!' and after a moment's thought I added; 'anyway, she's not his sister.'

VI

A WHOLE fortnight passed by. I visited the Gagins every day. Acia seemed to avoid me, but she did not permit herself one of the mischievous tricks which had so surprised me the first two days of our acquaintance. She seemed secretly wounded or embarrassed; she even laughed less than at first. I watched her with curiosity.

She spoke French and German fairly well; but one could easily see, in everything she did, that she had not from childhood been brought up under a woman's care, and that she had had a curious, irregular education that had nothing in common with Gagin's bringing up. He was, in spite of the Vandyck hat and the blouse, so thoroughly every inch of him the soft, half-effeminate Great Russian nobleman, while she was not like the young girl of the same class. In all her movements there was a certain restlessness. The wild stock had not long been grafted, the new wine was still fermenting. By nature modest and timid, she was exasperated by her own shyness, and in her exasperation tried to force herself to be bold and free and easy, in which she was not always successful. I sometimes began to talk to her about her life in Russia, about her past; she answered my questions reluctantly. I found out, however, that before going abroad she had lived a long while in the country. I came upon her once, intent on a book, alone. With her head on her hands and her fingers thrust into her hair, she was eagerly devouring the lines.

'Bravo!' I said, going up to her; 'how studious you are!' She raised her head, and looked gravely and severely at me. 'You think I can do nothing but laugh,' she said, and was about to go away. . . .

I glanced at the title of the book; it was some French novel.

'I can't commend your choice, though,' I observed.

'What am I to read then?' she cried; and flinging the book on the table, she added—'so I'd better go and play the fool,' and ran out into the garden.

That same day, in the evening, I was reading Gagin *Hermann und Dorothea*. Acia at first kept fidgeting about us, then all at once she stopped, listened, softly sat down by me, and heard the reading through to the end. The next day I hardly knew her again, till I guessed it had suddenly occurred to her to be as domestic and discreet as Dorothea. In fact I saw her as a half-enigmatic creature. Vain, self-conscious to the last degree, she attracted me even when I was irritated by her. Of one thing only I felt more and more convinced; and that was, that she was not Gagin's sister. His manner with her was not like a brother's, it was too affectionate, too considerate, and at the same time a little constrained.

A curious incident apparently confirmed my suspicions.

One evening, when I reached the vineyard where the Gagins lived, I found the gate fastened. Without losing much time in deliberation, I made my way to a broken-down place I had noticed before in the hedge and jumped over it. Not far from this spot there was a little arbour of acacias on one side of the path. I got up to it and was just about to pass it. . . . Suddenly I was struck by Acia's voice passionately and tearfully uttering the following words:

'No, I'll love no one but you, no, no, I will love you only, for ever!'

'Come, Acia, calm yourself,' said Gagin, 'you know I believe you.'

Their voices came from the arbour. I could see them both through the thin net-work of leaves. They did not notice me.

'You, you only,' she repeated, and she flung herself on his neck, and with broken sobs began kissing him and clinging to his breast.

'Come, come,' he repeated, lightly passing his hand over her hair.

For a few instants I stood motionless . . . Suddenly I started—should I go up to them? —'On no consideration,' flashed through my head. With rapid footsteps I turned back to the hedge, leaped over it into the road, and almost running, went home. I smiled, rubbed my hands, wondered at the chance which had so suddenly confirmed my surmises (I did not for one instant doubt their accuracy) and yet there was a great bitterness in my heart. What accomplished hypocrites they are, though, I thought. And what for? Why should he try to take me in? I shouldn't have expected it of him . . . And what a touching scene of reconciliation!

VII

I SLEPT badly, and next morning got up early, fastened a knapsack on my back, and telling my landlady not to expect me back for the night, set off walking to the mountains, along the upper part of the stream on which Z. is situated. These mountains, offsets of the ridge known as the Hundsrück, are very interesting from a geological point of view. They are especially remarkable for the purity and regularity of the strata of basalt; but I was in no mood for geological observations. I did not take stock of what was passing within me. One feeling was clear to me; a disinclination to see the Gagins. I assured myself that the sole reason of my sudden distaste for their society was anger at their duplicity. Who forced them to pass themselves off as brother and sister? However, I tried not to think about them; I sauntered in leisurely fashion about the mountains and valleys, sat in the village inns, talking peacefully to the innkeepers and people drinking in them, or lay on a flat stone warmed by the sun, and watched the clouds floating by.

Luckily it was exquisite weather. In such pursuits I passed three days, and not without pleasure, though my heart did ache at times. My own mood was in perfect harmony with the peaceful nature of that quiet countryside.

I gave myself up entirely to the play of circumstances, of fleeting impressions; in slow succession they flowed through my soul, and left on it at last one general sensation, in which all I had seen, felt, and heard in those three days was mingled—all; the delicate fragrance of resin in the forest, the call and tap of the woodpeckers, the never-ceasing chatter of the clear brooks, with spotted trout lying in the sand at the bottom, the somewhat softened outlines of the mountains, the surly rocks, the little clean villages, with respectable old churches and trees, the storks in the meadows, the neat mills with swiftly turning wheels, the beaming faces of the villagers, their blue smocks and grey stockings, the creaking, deliberately-moving wagons, drawn by sleek horses, and sometimes cows, the long-haired young men, wandering on the clean roads, planted with apple and pear trees. . . .

Even now I like to recall my impressions of those days. Good luck go with thee, modest nook of Germany, with thy simple plenty, with traces everywhere of busy hands, of patient though leisurely toil. . . . Good luck and peace to thee!

I came home at the end of the third day; I forgot to say that in my anger with the Gagins I tried to revive the image of my cruel-hearted widow, but my efforts were fruitless. I remember when I applied myself to musing upon her, I saw a little peasant girl of five years old, with a round little face and innocently staring eyes. She gazed with such childish directness at me. . . . I felt ashamed before her innocent stare, I could not lie in her presence, and at once, and once for all, said a last good-bye to my former flame.

At home I found a note from Gagin. He wondered at the suddenness of my plan, reproached me, asked why I had not taken him with me, and pressed me to go and see him directly I was back. I read this note with dissatisfaction ; but the next day I set off to the Gagins.

VIII

GAGIN met me in friendly fashion, and over-whelmed me with affectionate reproaches ; but Acia, as though intentionally, burst out laugh-ing for no reason whatever, directly she saw me, and promptly ran away, as she so often did. Gagin was disconcerted ; he muttered after her that she must be crazy, and begged me to excuse her. I confess I was very much annoyed with Acia ; already, apart from that, I was not at my ease ; and now again this unnatural laughter, these strange grimaces. I pretended, however, not to notice anything, and began telling Gagin some of the incidents of my short tour. He told me what he had been doing in my absence. But our talk did not flow easily ; Acia came into the room and ran out again ; I declared at last that I had urgent work to do, and must get back home. Gagin at first tried to keep me, then, looking intently at me, offered to see me on my way. In the passage, Acia suddenly came up to me and held out her hand ; I shook her fingers very slightly, and barely bowed to her. Gagin

263

and I crossed the Rhine together, and when we reached my favourite ash-tree with the statuette of the Madonna, we sat down on the bench to admire the view. A remarkable conversation took place between us.

At first we exchanged a few words, then we were silent, watching the clear river.

'Tell me,' began Gagin all at once, with his habitual smile, 'what do you think of Acia? I suppose she must strike you as rather strange, doesn't she?'

'Yes,' I answered, in some perplexity. I had not expected he would begin to speak of her.

'One has to know her well to judge of her,' he observed; 'she has a very good heart, but she's wilful. She's difficult to get on with. But you couldn't blame her if you knew her story. . . .'

'Her story?' I broke in. . . . 'Why, isn't she your——' Gagin glanced at me.

'Do you really think she isn't my sister? . . . No,' he went on, paying no attention to my confusion, 'she really is my sister, she's my father's daughter. Let me tell you about her, I feel I can trust you, and I'll tell you all about it.

'My father was very kind, clever, cultivated, and unhappy. Fate treated him no worse than others; but he could not get over her first blow. He married early, for love; his wife, my mother, died very soon after; I was only six months

old then. My father took me away with him
to his country place, and for twelve years he
never went out anywhere. He looked after
my education himself, and would never have
parted with me, if his brother, my uncle, had
not come to see us in the country. This uncle
always lived in Petersburg, where he held a
very important post. He persuaded my father
to put me in his charge, as my father would
not on any consideration agree to leave the
country. My uncle represented to him that it
was bad for a boy of my age to live in complete
solitude, that with such a constantly depressed
and taciturn instructor as my father I should
infallibly be much behind other boys of my
age in education, and that my character even
might very possibly suffer. My father resisted
his brother's counsels a long while, but he gave
way at last. I cried at parting from my father ;
I loved him, though I had never seen a smile
on his face . . . but when I got to Petersburg,
I soon forgot our dark and cheerless home. I
entered a cadet's school, and from school passed
on into a regiment of the Guards. Every
year I used to go home to the country for a
few weeks, and every year I found my father
more and more low-spirited, absorbed in himself, depressed, and even timorous. He used
to go to church every day, and had quite
got out of the way of talking. On one of my
visits—I was about twenty then—I saw for the

first time in our house a thin, dark-eyed little
girl of ten years old—Acia. My father told
me she was an orphan whom he had kept out
of charity—that was his very expression. I
paid no particular attention to her; she was
shy, quick in her movements, and silent as a
little wild animal, and directly I went into my
father's favourite room—an immense gloomy
apartment, where my mother had died, and
where candles were kept burning even in the
daytime—she would hide at once behind his
big arm-chair, or behind the book-case. It so
happened that for three or four years after that
visit the duties of the service prevented my
going home to the country. I used to get a
short letter from my father every month; Acia
he rarely mentioned, and only incidentally.
He was over fifty, but he seemed still young.
Imagine my horror; all of a sudden, suspecting
nothing, I received a letter from the steward,
in which he informed me my father was danger-
ously ill, and begged me to come as soon as
possible if I wanted to take leave of him. I
galloped off post-haste, and found my father
still alive, but almost at his last gasp. He
was greatly relieved to see me, clasped me in
his wasted arms, and gazed at me with a
long, half-scrutinising, half-imploring look, and
making me promise I would carry out his
last request, he told his old valet to bring
Acia. The old man brought her in; she could

scarcely stand upright, and was shaking all over.

'"Here," said my father with an effort, "I confide to you my daughter—your sister. You will hear all about her from Yakov," he added, pointing to the valet.

'Acia sobbed, and fell with her face on the bed. . . . Half-an-hour later my father died.

'This was what I learned. Acia was the daughter of my father by a former maid-servant of my mother's, Tatiana. I have a vivid recollection of this Tatiana, I remember her tall, slender figure, her handsome, stern, clever face, with big dark eyes. She had the character of being a proud, unapproachable girl. As far as I could find out from Yakov's respectful, unfinished sentences, my father had become attached to her some years after my mother's death. Tatiana was not living then in my father's house, but in the hut of a married sister, who had charge of the cows. My father became exceedingly fond of her, and after my departure from the country he even wanted to marry her, but she herself would not consent to be his wife, in spite of his entreaties.

'"The deceased Tatiana Vassilievna," Yakov informed me, standing in the doorway with his hands behind him, "had good sense in everything, and she didn't want to do harm to your father. 'A poor wife I should be for you, a poor sort of lady I should make,' so she was pleased to say, she said so before me." Tatiana would not even move into the house, and went on living at her sister's with Acia. In my childhood I used to see Tatiana only on saints' days in church. With her head tied up in a dark kerchief, and a yellow shawl on her shoulders, she used to stand in the crowd, near a window—her stern profile used to stand out sharply against the transparent window-pane—and she used to pray sedately and gravely, bowing low to the ground in the old-fashioned way. When my uncle carried me off, Acia was only two years old, and she lost her mother when she was nine.

'Directly Tatiana died, my father took Acia into his house. He had before then expressed a wish to have her with him, but that too Tatiana had refused him. Imagine what must have passed in Acia's mind when she was taken into the master's house. To this day she cannot forget the moment when they first put her on a silk dress and kissed her hand. Her mother, as long as she lived, had brought her up very strictly; with my father she enjoyed absolute freedom. He was her tutor; she saw no one except him. He did not spoil her, that is to say, he didn't fondle and pet her; but he loved her passionately, and never checked her in anything; in his heart he considered he had wronged her. Acia soon realised that she was the chief personage in the house; she knew the master was

her father ; but just as quickly she was aware
of her false position ; self-consciousness was
strongly developed in her, mistrustfulness too ;
bad habits took root, simplicity was lost. She
wanted (she confessed this to me once herself),
to force *the whole world* to forget her origin ;
she was ashamed of her mother, and at the
same time ashamed of being ashamed, and was
proud of her too. You see she knew and
knows a lot that she oughtn't to have known
at her age. . . . But was it her fault? The
forces of youth were at work in her, her heart
was in a ferment, and not a guiding hand near
her. Absolute independence in everything !
And wasn't it hard for her to put up with ?
She wanted to be as good as other young
ladies ; she flew to books. But what good
could she get from that ? Her life went on as
irregularly as it had begun, but her heart was
not spoiled, her intellect was uninjured.

'And there was I left, a boy of twenty, with
a girl of thirteen on my hands ! For the first
few days after my father's death the very sound
of my voice threw her into a fever, my caresses
caused her anguish, and it was only slowly and
gradually that she got used to me. It is true
that later, when she fully realised that I really
did acknowledge her as my sister, and cared for
her, she became passionately attached to me ;
she can feel nothing by halves.

'I took her to Petersburg. Painful as it was

to part with her, we could not live together. I sent her to one of the best boarding-schools. Acia knew our separation was inevitable, yet she began by fretting herself ill over it, and almost died. Later on she plucked up more spirit, and spent four years at school; but, contrary to my expectations, she was almost exactly the same as before. The headmistress of the school often made complaints of her, 'And we can't punish her,' she used to say to me, 'and she's not amenable to kindness.' Acia was exceedingly quick-witted, and did better at her lessons than any one; but she never would put herself on a level with the rest; she was perverse, and held herself aloof. . . . I could not blame her very much for it; in her position she had either to be subservient, or to hold herself aloof. Of all her school-fellows she only made friends with one, an ugly girl of poor family, who was sat upon by the rest. The other girls with whom she was brought up, mostly of good family, did not like her, teased her and taunted her as far as they could. Acia would not give way to them an inch. One day at their lesson on the law of God, the teacher was talking of the vices. 'Servility and cowardice are the worst vices,' Acia said aloud. She would still go her own way, in fact; only her manners were improved, though even in that respect I think she did not gain a great deal.

'At last she reached her seventeenth year. I could not keep her any longer at school. I found myself in a rather serious difficulty. Suddenly a blessed idea came to me—to resign my commission and go abroad for a year or two, taking Acia with me. No sooner thought than done; and here we are on the banks of the Rhine, where I am trying to take up painting, and she . . . is as naughty and troublesome as ever. But now I hope you will not judge her too harshly; for though she pretends she doesn't care, she values the good opinion of every one, and yours particularly.'

And Gagin smiled again his gentle smile. I pressed his hand warmly.

'That's how it is,' Gagin began again; 'but I have a trying time with her. She's like gunpowder, always ready to go off. So far, she has never taken a fancy to any one, but woe betide us, if she falls in love! I sometimes don't know what to do with her. The other day she took some notion into her head, and suddenly began declaring I was colder to her than I used to be, that she loved me and no one else, and never would love any one else. . . . And she cried so, as she said it—'

'So that was it,'—I was beginning, but I bit my tongue.

'Tell me,' I questioned Gagin, 'we have talked so frankly about everything, is it possible really, she has never cared for any one yet?

Didn't she see any young men in Petersburg?'

'She didn't like them at all. No, Acia wants a hero—an exceptional individual—or a picturesque shepherd on a mountain pass. But I've been chattering away, and keeping you,' he added, getting up.

'Do you know——,' I began ; 'let's go back to your place, I don't want to go home.'

'What about your work?'

I made no reply. Gagin smiled good-humouredly, and we went back to L. As I caught sight of the familiar vineyard and little white house, I felt a certain sweetness—yes, sweetness in my heart, as though honey was stealthily dropping thence for me. My heart was light after what Gagin had told me.

IX

ACIA met us in the very doorway of the house. I expected a laugh again; but she came to meet us, pale and silent, with downcast eyes.

'Here he is again,' Gagin began, 'and he wanted to come back of his own accord, observe.'

Acia looked at me inquiringly. It was my turn now to hold out my hand, and this time I pressed her chilly fingers warmly. I felt very sorry for her. I understood now a great deal in her that had puzzled me before; her inward restlessness, her want of breeding, her desire to be striking—all became clear to me. I had had a peep into that soul; a secret scourge was always tormenting her, her ignorant self-consciousness struggled in confused alarm, but her whole nature strove towards truth. I understood why this strange little girl attracted me; it was not only by the half-wild charm of her slender body that she attracted me; I liked her soul.

Gagin began rummaging among his canvases. I suggested to Acia that she should take a turn with me in the vineyard. She agreed at once, with cheerful and almost humble readiness. We went half-way down the mountain, and sat down on a broad stone.

'And you weren't dull without us?' Acia began.

'And were you dull without me?' I queried.

Acia gave me a sidelong look.

'Yes,' she answered. 'Was it nice in the mountains?' she went on at once. 'Were they high ones? Higher than the clouds? Tell me what you saw. You were telling my brother, but I didn't hear anything.'

'It was of your own accord you went away,' I remarked.

'I went away . . . because . . .—I'm not going away now,' she added with a confiding caress in her voice. 'You were angry to-day.'

'I?'

'Yes, you.'

'Upon my word, whatever for?'

'I don't know, but you were angry, and you went away angry. I was very much vexed that you went away like that, and I'm so glad you came back.'

'And I'm glad I came back,' I observed.

Acia gave herself a little shrug, as children often do when they are very pleased.

'Oh, I'm good at guessing!' she went on. 'Sometimes, simply from the way papa coughed,

I could tell in the next room whether he was pleased with me or not.'

Till that day Acia had never once spoken to me of her father. I was struck by it.

'Were you fond of your father?' I said, and suddenly, to my intense annoyance, I felt I was reddening.

She made no answer, and blushed too. We were both silent. In the distance a smoking steamer was scudding along on the Rhine. We began watching it.

'Why don't you tell me about your tour?' Acia murmured.

'Why did you laugh to-day directly you saw me?' I asked.

'I don't know really. Sometimes I want to cry, but I laugh. You mustn't judge me—by what I do. Oh, by-the-bye, what a story that is about the Lorelei! Is that *her* rock we can see? They say she used to drown every one, but as soon as she fell in love she threw herself in the water. I like that story. Frau Luise tells me all sorts of stories. Frau Luise has a black cat with yellow eyes. . . .'

Acia raised her head and shook her curls.

'Ah, I am happy,' she said.

At that instant there floated across to us broken, monotonous sounds. Hundreds of voices in unison and at regular intervals were repeating a chanted litany. The crowd of pilgrims

275

moved slowly along the road below with crosses and banners. . . .

'I should like to go with them,' said Acia, listening to the sounds of the voices gradually growing fainter.

'Are you so religious?'

'I should like to go far away on a pilgrimage, on some great exploit,' she went on. 'As it is, the days pass by, life passes by, and what have we done?'

'You are ambitious,' I observed. 'You want to live to some purpose, to leave some trace behind you. . . .'

'Is that impossible, then?'

'Impossible,' I was on the point of repeating. . . . But I glanced at her bright eyes, and only said:

'You can try.'

'Tell me,' began Acia, after a brief silence during which shadows passed over her face, which had already turned pale, 'did you care much for that lady? . . . You remember my brother drank her health at the ruins the day after we first knew you.'

I laughed.

'Your brother was joking. I never cared for any lady; at any rate, I don't care for one now.'

'And what do you like in women?' she asked, throwing back her head with innocent curiosity.

'What a strange question!' I cried.

Acia was a little disconcerted.

'I ought not to ask you such a question, ought I? Forgive me, I'm used to chattering away about anything that comes into my head. That's why I'm afraid to speak.'

'Speak, for God's sake, don't be afraid,' I hastened to intervene; 'I'm so glad you're leaving off being shy at last.'

Acia looked down, and laughed a soft light-hearted laugh; I had never heard such a laugh from her.

'Well, tell me about something,' she went on, stroking out the skirt of her dress, and arranging the folds over her legs, as though she were settling herself for a long while; 'tell me or read me something, just as you read us, do you remember, from *Oniegin* . . .'

She suddenly grew pensive—

'Where now is the cross and the branches' shade
  Over my poor mother's grave !'

She murmured in a low voice.

'That's not as it is in Pushkin,' I observed.

'But I should like to have been Tatiana,' she went on, in the same dreamy tone. 'Tell me a story,' she suddenly added eagerly.

But I was not in a mood for telling stories. I was watching her, all bathed in the bright sunshine, all peace and gentleness. Everything was joyously radiant about us, below, and above us—sky, earth, and waters; the very air seemed saturated with brilliant light.

'Look, how beautiful!' I said, unconsciously sinking my voice.

'Yes, it is beautiful,' she answered just as softly, not looking at me. 'If only you and I were birds—how we would soar, how we would fly. . . . We'd simply plunge into that blue . . . But we're not birds.'

'But we may grow wings,' I rejoined.

'How so?'

'Live a little longer—and you'll find out. There are feelings that lift us above the earth. Don't trouble yourself, you will have wings.'

'Have you had them?'

'How shall I say . . . I think up till now I never have taken flight.'

Acia grew pensive once more. I bent a little towards her.

'Can you waltz?' she asked me suddenly.

'Yes,' I answered, rather puzzled.

'Well, come along then, come along . . . I'll ask my brother to play us a waltz. . . . We'll fancy we are flying, that our wings have grown.'

She ran into the house. I ran after her, and in a few minutes, we were turning round and round the narrow little room, to the sweet strains of Lanner. Acia waltzed splendidly, with enthusiasm. Something soft and womanly suddenly peeped through the childish severity of her profile. Long after, my arm kept the feeling of the contact of her soft waist, long after I heard her quickened breathing close to my ear, long after I was haunted by dark, immobile, almost closed eyes in a pale but eager face, framed in by fluttering curls.

X

ALL that day passed most delightfully. We were as merry as children. Acia was very sweet and simple. Gagin was delighted, as he watched her. I went home late. When I had got out into the middle of the Rhine, I asked the ferryman to let the boat float down with the current. The old man pulled up his oars, and the majestic river bore us along. As I looked about me, listened, brooded over recollections, I was suddenly aware of a secret restlessness astir in my heart . . . I lifted my eyes skywards, but there was no peace even in the sky; studded with stars, it seemed all moving, quivering, twinkling; I bent over to the river—but even there, even in those cold dark depths, the stars were trembling and glimmering; I seemed to feel an exciting quickening of life on all sides—and a sense of alarm rose up within me too. I leaned my elbows on the boat's edge . . . The whispering of the wind in my ears, the soft gurgling of the water at the rudder worked on my nerves, and the fresh breath of the river did not cool me;

a nightingale was singing on the bank, and stung me with the sweet poison of its notes. Tears rose into my eyes, but they were not the tears of aimless rapture. . . . What I was feeling was not the vague sense I had known of late of all-embracing desire when the soul expands, resounds, when it feels that it grasps all, loves all. . . . No! it was the thirst for happiness aflame in me. I did not dare yet to call it by its name—but happiness, happiness full and overflowing—that was what I wanted, that was what I pined for. . . . The boat floated on, and the old ferryman sat dozing as he leant on his oars.

XI

As I set off next day to the Gagins, I did not ask myself whether I was in love with Acia, but I thought a great deal about her, her fate absorbed me, I rejoiced at our unexpected intimacy. I felt that it was only yesterday I had got to know her; till then she had turned away from me. And now, when she had at last revealed herself to me, in what a seductive light her image showed itself, how fresh it was for me, what secret fascinations were modestly peeping out. . . .

I walked boldly up the familiar road, gazing continually at the cottage, a white spot in the distance. I thought not of the future—not even of the morrow—I was very happy.

Acia flushed directly I came into the room; I noticed that she had dressed herself in her best again, but the expression of her face was not in keeping with her finery; it was mournful. And I had come in such high spirits! I even fancied that she was on the point of running away as usual, but she controlled herself and remained. Gagin was in that peculiar condition of artistic heat and intensity which seizes amateurs all of a sudden, like a fit, when they imagine they are succeeding in 'catching nature and pinning her down.' He was standing with dishevelled locks, and besmeared with paint, before a stretched canvas, and flourishing the brush over it; he almost savagely nodded to me, turned away, screwed up his eyes, and bent again over his picture. I did not hinder him, but went and sat down by Acia. Slowly her dark eyes turned to me.

'You're not the same to-day as yesterday,' I observed, after ineffectual efforts to call up a smile on her lips.

'No, I'm not,' she answered, in a slow and dull voice. 'But that means nothing. I did not sleep well, I was thinking all night.'

'What about?'

'Oh, I thought about so many things. It's a way I have had from childhood; ever since I used to live with mother—'

She uttered the word with an effort, and then repeated again—

'When I used to live with mother . . . I used to think why it was no one could tell what would happen to him; and sometimes one sees trouble coming—and one can't escape; and how it is one can never tell all the truth . . . Then I used to think I knew nothing, and that I ought to learn. I want to be educated over again; I'm very badly educated. I can't play the piano, I can't draw, and even sewing I do very badly. I have no talent for anything; I must be a very dull person to be with.'

'You're unjust to yourself,' I replied; 'you've read a lot, you're cultivated, and with your cleverness—'

'Why, am I clever?' she asked with such naïve interest, that I could not help laughing; but she did not even smile. 'Brother, am I clever?' she asked Gagin.

He made her no answer, but went on working, continually changing brushes and raising his arm.

'I don't know myself what is in my head,' Acia continued, with the same dreamy air. 'I am sometimes afraid of myself, really. Ah, I should like . . . Is it true that women ought not to read a great deal?'

'A great deal's not wanted, but . . .'

'Tell me what I ought to read? Tell me what I ought to do. I will do everything you tell me,' she added, turning to me with innocent confidence.

I could not at once find a reply.

'You won't be dull with me, though?'

'What nonsense,' I was beginning. . . .

'All right, thanks!' Acia put in; 'I was thinking you would be bored.'

And her little hot hand clasped mine warmly.

'N!' Gagin cried at that instant; 'isn't that background too dark?'

I went up to him. Acia got up and went away.

XII

SHE came back in an hour, stood in the door-way and beckoned to me.

'Listen,' she said; 'if I were to die, would you be sorry?'

'What ideas you have to-day!' I exclaimed.

'I fancy I shall die soon; it seems to me sometimes as though everything about me were saying good-bye. It's better to die than live like this. . . . Ah! don't look at me like that; I'm not pretending, really. Or else I shall begin to be afraid of you again.'

'Why, were you afraid of me?'

'If I am queer, it's really not my fault,' she rejoined. 'You see, I can't even laugh now. . . .'

She remained gloomy and preoccupied till evening. Something was taking place in her; what, I did not understand. Her eyes often rested upon me; my heart slowly throbbed under her enigmatic gaze. She appeared com-posed, and yet as I watched her I kept wanting to tell her not to let herself get excited. I admired her, found a touching charm in her pale face, her hesitating, slow movements, but she for some reason fancied I was out of humour.

'Let me tell you something,' she said to me not long before parting; 'I am tortured by the idea that you consider me frivolous. . . . For the future believe what I say to you, only do you, too, be open with me; and I will always tell you the truth, I give you my word of honour. . . .'

This 'word of honour' set me laughing again.

'Oh, don't laugh,' she said earnestly, 'or I shall say to you to-day what you said to me yesterday, "why are you laughing?"' and after a brief silence she added, 'Do you remember you spoke yesterday of "wings"? . . . My wings have grown, but I have nowhere to fly.'

'Nonsense,' I said; 'all the ways lie open before you. . . .'

Acia looked at me steadily, straight in the face.

'You have a bad opinion of me to-day,' she said, frowning.

'I? a bad opinion of you! . . .'

'Why is it you are both so low-spirited,' Gagin interrupted me—'would you like me to play a waltz, as I did yesterday?'

'No, no,' replied Acia, and she clenched her hands; 'not to-day, not for anything!'

'I'm not going to force you to; don't excite yourself.'

'Not for anything!' she repeated, turning pale.

'Can it be she's in love with me?' I thought, as I drew near the dark rushing waters of the Rhine.

XIII

'Can it be that she loves me?' I asked myself next morning, directly I awoke. I did not want to look into myself. I felt that her image, the image of the 'girl with the affected laugh,' had crept close into my heart, and that I should not easily get rid of it. I went to L—— and stayed there the whole day, but I saw Acia only by glimpses. She was not well; she had a headache. She came downstairs for a minute, with a bandage round her forehead, looking white and thin, her eyes half-closed. With a faint smile she said, 'It will soon be over, it 's nothing; everything 's soon over, isn't it?' and went away. I felt bored and, as it were, listlessly sad, yet I could not make up my mind to go for a long while, and went home late, without seeing her again.

The next morning passed in a sort of half slumber of the consciousness. I tried to set to work, and could not; I tried to do nothing and not to think—and that was a failure too. I strolled about the town, returned home, went out again.

'Are you Herr N——?' I heard a childish voice ask suddenly behind me. I looked round; a little boy was standing before me. 'This is for you from Fraülein Annette,' he said, handing me a note.

I opened it and recognised the irregular rapid handwriting of Acia. 'I must see you to-day,' she wrote to me; 'come to-day at four o'clock to the stone chapel on the road near the ruin. I have done a most foolish thing to-day. . . . Come, for God's sake; you shall know all about it. . . . Tell the messenger, yes.'

'Is there an answer?' the boy asked me.

'Say, yes,' I replied. The boy ran off.

XIV

I went home to my own room, sat down, and sank into thought. My heart was beating violently. I read Acia's note through several times. I looked at my watch; it was not yet twelve o'clock.

The door opened, Gagin walked in.

His face was overcast. He seized my hand and pressed it warmly. He seemed very much agitated.

'What is the matter?' I asked.

Gagin took a chair and sat down opposite me. 'Three days ago,' he began with a rather forced smile, and hesitating, 'I surprised you by what I told you; to-day I am going to surprise you more. With any other man I could not, most likely, bring myself . . . so directly. . . . But you're an honourable man, you're my friend, aren't you? Listen—my sister, Acia, is in love with you.'

I trembled all over and stood up. . . .

'Your sister, you say——'

'Yes, yes,' Gagin cut me short. 'I tell you, she's mad, and she'll drive me mad. But happily she can't tell a lie, and she confides in me. Ah, what a soul there is in that little girl! . . . but she'll be her own ruin, that's certain.'

'But you're making a mistake,' I began.

'No, I'm not making a mistake. Yesterday, you know, she was lying down almost all day, she ate nothing, but she did not complain. . . . She never does complain. I was not anxious, though towards evening she was in a slight fever. At two o'clock last night I was wakened by our landlady; "Go to your sister," she said; "there's something wrong with her." I ran in to Acia, and found her not undressed, feverish, and in tears; her head was aching, her teeth were chattering. "What's the matter with you?" I said, "are you ill?" She threw herself on my neck and began imploring me to take her away as soon as possible, if I want to keep her alive. . . . I could make out nothing, I tried to soothe her. . . . Her sobs grew more violent, . . . and suddenly through her sobs I made out . . . well, in fact, I made out that she loves you. I assure you, you and I are reasonable people, and we can't imagine how deeply she feels and with what incredible force her feelings show themselves; it has come upon her as unexpectedly and irresistibly as a thunderstorm. You're a very nice person,' Gagin pursued, 'but why she's so in love with you, I confess I don't understand. She says she has been drawn to you from the first moment she saw you. That's why she cried the other day when she declared she would never love any one but me.—She imagines you despise her, that you most likely know about her birth; she asked me if I hadn't told you her story,—I said, of course, that I hadn't; but her intuition's simply terrible. She has one wish,—to get away, to get away at once. I sat with her till morning; she made me promise we should not be here to-morrow, and only then, she fell asleep. I have been thinking and thinking, and at last I made up my mind to speak to you. To my mind, Acia is right; the best thing is for us both to go away from here. And I should have taken her away to-day, if I had not been struck by an idea which made me pause. Perhaps . . . who knows? do you like my sister? If so, what's the object of my taking her away? And so I decided to cast aside all reserve. . . . Besides, I noticed something myself . . . I made up my mind . . . to find out from you . . .' Poor Gagin was completely out of countenance. 'Excuse me, please,' he added, 'I'm not used to such bothers.'

I took his hand.

'You want to know,' I pronounced in a steady voice, 'whether I like your sister? Yes, I do like her—'

Gagin glanced at me. 'But,' he said,

faltering, 'you'd hardly marry her, would you?'

'How would you have me answer such a question? Only think; can I at the moment——'

'I know, I know,' Gagin cut me short; 'I have no right to expect an answer from you, and my question was the very acme of impropriety. . . . But what am I to do? One can't play with fire. You don't know Acia; she's quite capable of falling ill, running away, or asking you to see her alone. . . . Any other girl might manage to hide it all and wait—but not she. It is the first time with her, that's the worst of it! If you had seen how she sobbed at my feet to-day, you would understand my fears.'

I was pondering. Gagin's words 'asking you to see her alone,' had sent a twinge to my heart. I felt it was shameful not to meet his honest frankness with frankness.

'Yes,' I said at last; 'you are right. An hour ago I got a note from your sister. Here it is.'

Gagin took the note, quickly looked it through, and let his hands fall on his knees. The expression of perplexity on his face was very amusing, but I was in no mood for laughter.

'I tell you again, you're an honourable man,' he said; 'but what's to be done now? What? she herself wants to go away, and she writes

to you and blames herself for acting unwisely
. . . and when had she time to write this?
What does she wish of you?'

I pacified him, and we began to discuss as
coolly as we could what we ought to do.

The conclusion we reached at last was that,
to avoid worse harm befalling, I was to go and
meet Acia, and to have a straight-forward
explanation with her; Gagin pledged himself
to stay at home, and not to give a sign of
knowing about her note to me; in the evening
we arranged to see each other again.

'I have the greatest confidence in you,' said
Gagin, and he pressed my hand; 'have mercy
on her and on me. But we shall go away
to-morrow, anyway,' he added getting up, 'for
you won't marry Acia, I see.'

'Give me time till the evening,' I objected.

'All right, but you won't marry her.'

He went away, and I threw myself on the
sofa, and shut my eyes. My head was going
round; too many impressions had come bursting on it at once. I was vexed at Gagin's
frankness, I was vexed with Acia, her love
delighted and disconcerted me, I could not
comprehend what had made her reveal it to her
brother; the absolute necessity of rapid, almost
instantaneous decision exasperated me. 'Marry
a little girl of seventeen, with her character,
how is it possible?' I said, getting up.

XV

AT the appointed hour I crossed the Rhine, and the first person I met on the opposite bank was the very boy who had come to me in the morning. He was obviously waiting for me.

'From Fraülein Annette,' he said in a whisper, and he handed me another note.

Acia informed me she had changed the place of our meeting. I was to go in an hour and a half, not to the chapel, but to Frau Luise's house, to knock below, and go up to the third storey.

'Is it, yes, again?' asked the boy.

'Yes,' I repeated, and I walked along the bank of the Rhine. There was not time to go home, I didn't want to wander about the streets. Beyond the town wall there was a little garden, with a skittle ground and tables for beer drinkers. I went in there. A few middle-aged Germans were playing skittles ; the wooden balls rolled along with a sound of knocking, now and then cries of approval reached me. A pretty waitress, with her eyes swollen with weeping, brought me a tankard of

beer; I glanced at her face. She turned quickly
and walked away.

'Yes, yes,' observed a fat, red-cheeked citizen
sitting by, 'our Hannchen is dreadfully upset
to-day; her sweetheart's gone for a soldier.'
I looked at her; she was sitting huddled up in
a corner, her face propped on her hand; tears
were rolling one by one between her fingers.
Some one called for beer; she took him a pot,
and went back to her place. Her grief affected
me; I began musing on the interview awaiting
me, but my dreams were anxious, cheerless
dreams. It was with no light heart I was going
to this interview; I had no prospect before me
of giving myself up to the bliss of love returned;
what lay before me was to keep my word, to
do a difficult duty. 'One can't play with her.'
These words of Gagin's had gone through my
heart like arrows. And three days ago, in that
boat borne along by the current, had I not
been pining with the thirst for happiness? It
had become possible, and I was hesitating, I
was pushing it away, I was bound to push
it from me—its suddenness bewildered me.
Acia herself, with her fiery temperament, her
past, her bringing-up, this fascinating, strange
creature, I confess she frightened me. My
feelings were long struggling within me. The
appointed hour was drawing near. 'I can't
marry her,' I decided at last; 'she shall not
know I love her.'

I got up, and putting a thaler in the hand of poor Hannchen (she did not even thank me), I directed my steps towards Frau Luise's. The air was already overcast with the shadows of evening, and the narrow strip of sky, above the dark street, was red with the glow of sunset. I knocked faintly at the door; it was opened at once. I stepped through the doorway, and found myself in complete darkness.

'This way.' I heard an old woman's voice. 'You're expected.'

I took two steps, groping my way, a long hand took mine.

'Is that you, Frau Luise?' I asked.

'Yes,' answered the same voice, ''Tis I, my fine young man.' The old woman led me up a steep staircase, and stopped on the third floor. In the feeble light from a tiny window, I saw the wrinkled visage of the burgomaster's widow. A crafty smile of mawkish sweetness contorted her sunken lips, and pursed up her dim-sighted eyes. She pointed me to a little door; with an abrupt movement I opened it and slammed it behind me.

XVI

IN the little room into which I stepped, it was rather dark, and I did not at once see Acia. Wrapped in a big shawl, she was sitting on a chair by the window, turning away from me and almost hiding her head like a frightened bird. She was breathing quickly, and trembling all over. I felt unutterably sorry for her. I went up to her. She averted her head still more. . . .

'Anna Nikolaevna,' I said.

She suddenly drew herself up, tried to look at me, and could not. I took her hand, it was cold, and lay like a dead thing in mine.

'I wished'—Acia began, trying to smile, but unable to control her pale lips; 'I wanted —No, I can't,' she said, and ceased. Her voice broke at every word.

I sat down beside her.

'Anna Nikolaevna,' I repeated, and I too could say nothing more.

A silence followed. I still held her hand and looked at her. She sat as before, shrinking together, breathing with difficulty, and stealthily

biting her lower lip to keep back the rising tears.
. . . I looked at her ; there was something touchingly helpless in her timid passivity ; it seemed as though she had been so exhausted she had hardly reached the chair, and had simply fallen on it. My heart began to melt . . .

'Acia,' I said hardly audibly . . .

She slowly lifted her eyes to me. . . . Oh, the eyes of a woman who loves—who can describe them ? They were supplicating, those eyes, they were confiding, questioning, surrendering . . . I could not resist their fascination. A subtle flame passed all through me with tingling shocks ; I bent down and pressed my lips to her hand. . . .

I heard a quivering sound, like a broken sigh and I felt on my hair the touch of a feeble hand shaking like a leaf. I raised my head and looked at her face. How transformed it was all of a sudden. The expression of terror had vanished from it, her eyes looked far away and drew me after them, her lips were slightly parted, her forehead was white as marble, and her curls floated back as though the wind had stirred them. I forgot everything, I drew her to me, her hand yielded unresistingly, her whole body followed her hand, the shawl fell from her shoulders, and her head lay softly on my breast, lay under my burning lips. . . .

'Yours' . . . she murmured, hardly above a breath.

My arms were slipping round her waist. . . .
But suddenly the thought of Gagin flashed like
lightning before me. 'What are we doing,' I
cried, abruptly moving back . . . 'Your brother
. . . why, he knows everything. . . . He knows
I am with you.'

Acia sank back on her chair.

'Yes,' I went on, getting up and walking to
the other end of the room. 'Your brother
knows all about it . . . I had to tell him.' . . .

'You had to?' she articulated thickly. She
could not, it seemed, recover herself, and hardly
understood me.

'Yes, yes,' I repeated with a sort of exasperation, 'and it's all your fault, your fault. What
did you betray your secret for? Who forced
you to tell your brother? He has been with
me to-day, and told me what you said to him.'
I tried not to look at Acia, and kept walking
with long strides up and down the room. 'Now
everything is over, everything.'

Acia tried to get up from her chair.

'Stay,' I cried, 'stay, I implore you. You
have to do with an honourable man—yes, an
honourable man. But, in Heaven's name, what
upset you? Did you notice any change in
me? But I could not hide my feelings from
your brother when he came to me to-day.'

'Why am I talking like this?' I was thinking
inwardly, and the idea that I was an immoral
liar, that Gagin knew of our interview, that

everything was spoilt, exposed—seemed buzzing persistently in my head.

'I didn't call my brother'—I heard a frightened whisper from Acia: 'he came of himself.'

'See what you have done,' I persisted. 'Now you want to go away. . . .'

'Yes, I must go away,' she murmured in the same soft voice. 'I only asked you to come here to say good-bye.'

'And do you suppose,' I retorted, 'it will be easy for me to part with you?'

'But what did you tell my brother for?' Acia said, in perplexity.

'I tell you—I could not do otherwise. If you had not yourself betrayed yourself. . . .'

'I locked myself in my room,' she answered simply. 'I did not know the landlady had another key. . . .'

This innocent apology on her lips at such a moment almost infuriated me at the time . . . and now I cannot think of it without emotion. Poor, honest, truthful child!

'And now everything's at an end!' I began again, 'everything. Now we shall have to part.' I stole a look at Acia. . . . Her face had quickly flushed crimson. She was, I felt it, both ashamed and afraid. I went on walking and talking as though in delirium. 'You did not let the feeling develop which had begun to grow; you have broken off our relations yourself; you had no confidence in me; you doubted me. . . .'

While I was talking, Acia bent more and more forward, and suddenly slid on her knees, dropped her head on her arms, and began sobbing. I ran up to her and tried to lift her up, but she would not let me. I can't bear women's tears; at the sight of them I am at my wits' end at once.

'Anna Nikolaevna, Acia,' I kept repeating, 'please, I implore you, for God's sake, stop.' . . . I took her hand again. . . .

But, to my immense astonishment she suddenly jumped up, rushed with lightning swiftness to the door, and vanished. . . .

When, a few minutes later, Frau Luise came into the room I was still standing in the very middle of it, as it were, thunderstruck. I could not believe this interview could possibly have come to such a quick, such a stupid end, when I had not said a hundredth part of what I wanted to say, and what I ought to have said, when I did not know myself in what way it would be concluded. . . .

'Is Fraülein gone?' Frau Luise asked me, raising her yellow eyebrows right up to her false front.

I stared at her like a fool, and went away.

XVII

I MADE my way out of the town and struck out straight into the open country. I was devoured by anger, frenzied anger. I hurled reproaches at myself. How was it I had not seen the reason that had forced Acia to change the place of our meeting; how was it I did not appreciate what it must have cost her to go to that old woman; how was it I had not kept her? Alone with her, in that dim, half-dark room I had had the force, I had had the heart to repulse her, even to reproach her. ... Now her image simply pursued me. I begged her forgiveness. The thought of that pale face, those wet and timid eyes, of her loose hair falling on the drooping neck, the light touch of her head against my breast maddened me. 'Yours'—I heard her whisper. 'I acted from conscientious motives,' I assured myself. ... Not true! Did I really desire such a termination? Was I capable of parting from her? Could I really do without her?

'Madman! madman!' I repeated with exasperation. . . .

Meanwhile night was coming on. I walked with long strides towards the house where Acia lived.

XVIII

GAGIN came out to meet me

'Have you seen my sister?' he shouted to me while I was still some distance off.

'Why, isn't she at home? I asked.

'No.'

'She hasn't come back?'

'No. I was in fault,' Gagin went on. 'I couldn't restrain myself. Contrary to our agreement, I went to the chapel; she was not there; didn't she come, then?'

'She hasn't been at the chapel?'

'And you haven't seen her?'

I was obliged to admit I had seen her.

'Where?'

'At Frau Luise's. I parted from her an hour ago,' I added. 'I felt sure she had come home.'

'We will wait a little,' said Gagin.

We went into the house and sat down near each other. We were silent. We both felt very uncomfortable. We were continually looking round, staring at the door, listening. At last Gagin got up.

'Oh, this is beyond anything!' he cried. 'My

heart's in my mouth. She'll be the death of me, by God! . . . Let's go and look for her.'

We went out. It was quite dark by now, outside.

'What did you talk about to her?' Gagin asked me, as he pulled his hat over his eyes.

'I only saw her for five minutes,' I answered. 'I talked to her as we agreed.'

'Do you know what?' he replied, 'it's better for us to separate. In that way we are more likely to come across her before long. In any case come back here within an hour.'

XIX

I WENT hurriedly down from the vineyard
and rushed into the town. I walked rapidly
through all the streets, looked in all directions,
even at Frau Luise's windows, went back to the
Rhine, and ran along the bank. . . . From time
to time I was met by women's figures, but Acia
was nowhere to be seen. There was no anger
gnawing at my heart now. I was tortured by
a secret terror, and it was not only terror that
I felt . . . no, I felt remorse, the most intense
regret, and love,—yes! the tenderest love. I
wrung my hands. I called 'Acia' through the
falling darkness of the night, first in a low
voice, then louder and louder; I repeated a
hundred times over that I loved her. I vowed
I would never part from her. I would have
given everything in the world to hold her cold
hand again, to hear again her soft voice, to see
her again before me. . . . She had been so near,
she had come to me, her mind perfectly made
up, in perfect innocence of heart and feelings,
she had offered me her unsullied youth . . . and
I had not folded her to my breast, I had robbed

myself of the bliss of watching her sweet face blossom with delight and the peace of rapture. . . . This thought drove me out of my mind.

'Where can she have gone? What can she have done with herself?' I cried in an agony of helpless despair. . . . I caught a glimpse of something white on the very edge of the river. I knew the place; there stood there, over the tomb of a man who had been drowned seventy years ago, a stone cross half-buried in the ground, bearing an old inscription. My heart sank . . . I ran up to the cross; the white figure vanished. I shouted 'Acia!' I felt frightened myself by my uncanny voice, but no one called back.

I resolved to go and see whether Gagin had found her.

XX

As I climbed swiftly up the vineyard path I caught sight of a light in Acia's room. . . . This reassured me a little.

I went up to the house. The door below was fastened. I knocked. A window on the ground floor was cautiously opened, and Gagin's head appeared.

'Have you found her?' I asked.

'She has come back,' he answered in a whisper. 'She is in her own room undressing. Everything is all right.'

'Thank God!' I cried, in an indescribable rush of joy. 'Thank God! now everything is right. But you know we must have another talk.'

'Another time,' he replied, softly drawing the casement towards him. 'Another time; but now good-bye.'

'Till to-morrow,' I said. 'To-morrow everything shall be arranged.'

'Good-bye,' repeated Gagin. The window was closed. I was on the point of knocking at the window. I was on the point of telling

Gagin there and then that I wanted to ask him for his sister's hand. But such a proposal at such a time. . . . 'To-morrow,' I reflected, 'to-morrow I shall be happy. . . .'

To-morrow I shall be happy! Happiness has no to-morrow, no yesterday; it thinks not on the past, and dreams not of the future; it has the present—not a day even—a moment.

I don't remember how I got to Z. It was not my legs that carried me, nor a boat that ferried me across; I felt that I was borne along by great, mighty wings. I passed a bush where a nightingale was singing. I stopped and listened long; I fancied it sang my love and happiness.

XXI

WHEN next morning I began to approach the little house I knew so well, I was struck with one circumstance; all the windows in it were open, and the door too stood open; some bits of paper were lying about in front of the doorway; a maidservant appeared with a broom at the door.

I went up to her. . . .

'They are gone!' she bawled, before I had time to inquire whether Gagin was at home.

'Gone?' . . . I repeated. 'What do you mean by gone?   Where?'

'They went away this morning at six o'clock, and didn't say where. Wait a minute, I believe you're Mr. N——, aren't you?'

'I'm Mr. N——, yes.'

'The mistress has a letter for you.' The maid went up-stairs and returned with a letter. 'Here it is, if you please, sir.'

'But it's impossible. . . . how can it be?' . . . I was beginning. The servant stared blankly at me, and began sweeping.

I opened the letter. Gagin had written it;

there was not one word from Acia. He began
with begging me not to be angry at his sudden
departure; he felt sure that, on mature consideration, I should approve of his decision.
He could find no other way out of a position
which might become difficult and dangerous.
'Yesterday evening,' he wrote, 'while we were
both waiting in silence for Acia, I realised
conclusively the necessity of separation. There
are prejudices I respect; I can understand
that it's impossible for you to marry Acia.
She has told me everything; for the sake of
her peace of mind, I was bound to yield to her
reiterated urgent entreaties.' At the end of
the letter he expressed his regret that our
acquaintance had come to such a speedy
termination, wished me every happiness, shook
my hand in friendship, and besought me not to
try to seek them out.

'What prejudices?' I cried aloud, as though
he could hear me; 'what rubbish! What
right has he to snatch her from me? . . .' I
clutched at my head.

The servant began loudly calling for her
mistress; her alarm forced me to control myself. One idea was aflame within me; to find
them, to find them wherever they might be.
To accept this blow, to resign myself to such a
calamity was impossible. I learnt from the
landlady that they had got on to a steamer at
six o'clock in the morning, and were going

down the Rhine. I went to the ticket-office; there I was told they had taken tickets for Cologne. I was going home to pack up at once and follow them. I happened to pass the house of Frau Luise. . . . Suddenly I heard some one calling me. I raised my head, and at the window of the very room where I had met Acia the day before, I saw the burgomaster's widow. She smiled her loathsome smile, and called me. I turned away, and was going on; but she called after me that she had something for me. These words brought me to a halt, and I went into her house. How can I describe my feelings when I saw that room again? . . .

'By rights,' began the old woman, showing me a little note; 'I oughtn't to have given you this unless you'd come to me of your own accord, but you are such a fine young man. Take it.'

I took the note.

On a tiny scrap of paper stood the following words, hurriedly scribbled in pencil:

'Good-bye, we shall not see each other again. It is not through pride that I'm going away—no, I can't help it. Yesterday when I was crying before you, if you had said one word to me, only one word—I should have stayed. You did not say it. It seems it is better so . . . Good-bye for ever!'

One word . . . Oh, madman that I was!

314

That word . . . I had repeated it the night before with tears, I had flung it to the wind, I had said it over and over again among the empty fields . . . but I did not say it to her, I did not tell her I loved her . . . Indeed, I could not have uttered that word then. When I met her in that fatal room, I had as yet no clear consciousness of my love; it had not fully awakened even when I was sitting with her brother in senseless and burdensome silence . . . it flamed up with irrepressible force only a few instants later, when, terrified by the possibility of misfortune, I began to seek and call her . . . but then it was already too late. 'But that's impossible!' I shall be told; I don't know whether it's possible, I know that it's the truth. Acia would not have gone away if there had been the faintest shade of coquetry in her, and if her position had not been a false one. She could not put up with what any other girl would have endured; I did not realise that. My evil genius had arrested an avowal on my lips at my last interview with Gagin at the darkened window, and the last thread I might have caught at, had slipped out of my fingers.

The same day I went back with my portmanteau packed, to L., and started for Cologne. I remember the steamer was already off, and I was taking a mental farewell of those streets, all those spots which I was never to forget — when I caught sight of Hannchen. She was sitting on a seat near the river. Her face was pale but not sad ; a handsome young fellow was standing beside her, laughing and telling her some story ; while on the other side of the Rhine my little Madonna peeped out of the green of the old ash-tree as mournfully as ever.

XXII

In Cologne I came upon traces of the Gagins;
I found out they had gone to London; I
pushed on in pursuit of them; but in London
all my researches were in vain. It was long
before I would resign myself, for a long while
I persevered, but I was obliged, at last, to give
up all hope of coming across them.

And I never saw them again—I never saw
Acia. Vague rumours reached me about him,
but she had vanished for ever for me. I don't
even know whether she is alive. One day, a
few years later, in a railway carriage abroad,
I caught a glimpse of a woman, whose face
vividly recalled those features I could never
forget . . . but I was most likely deceived by
a chance resemblance. Acia remained in my
memory a little girl such as I had known her
at the best time of my life, as I saw her the
last time, leaning against the back of a low
wooden chair.

But I must own I did not grieve over-long
for her; I even came to the conclusion that
fate had done all for the best in not uniting

me to Acia; I consoled myself with the reflection that I should probably not have been
happy with such a wife. I was young then—
and the future, the brief, swiftly-passing future
seemed boundless to me then. Could not what
had been be repeated, I thought, and better,
fairer still? . . . I got to know other women—
but the feeling Acia had aroused in me, that
intense, tender, deep feeling has never come
again. No! no eyes have for me taken the
place of those that were once turned with love
upon my eyes, to no heart, pressed to my
breast, has my heart responded with such
joyous sweet emotion! Condemned as I have
been to a solitary life, without ties or family,
I have led a dreary existence; but I keep as
sacred relics, her little notes and the dry
geranium, the flower she threw me once out of
the window. It still retains a faint scent, while
the hand that gave it, the hand I only once
pressed to my lips, has perhaps long since
decayed in the grave . . . And I myself, what
has become of me? What is left of me, of
those blissful, heart-stirring days, of those
winged hopes and aspirations? The faint
fragrance of an insignificant plant outlives all
man's joys and sorrows—outlives man himself.

1857.